sending
in the

CLOWNS

To my friend,

* Jim *

— JKinai

5/7/14

sending in the CLOWNS

WRITTEN BY
KRIS RALSTON

TATE PUBLISHING & *Enterprises*

Published by Tate Publishing & Enterprises, LLC
127 E. Trade Center Terrace | Mustang, Oklahoma 73064 USA
1.888.361.9473 | www.tatepublishing.com

Tate Publishing is committed to excellence in the publishing industry. The company reflects the philosophy established by the founders, based on Psalm 68:11,
"The Lord gave the word and great was the company of those who published it."

Book design copyright © 2008 by Tate Publishing, LLC. All rights reserved.
Cover design by Jonathan Lindsay
Interior design by Stephanie Woloszyn

Published in the United States of America

ISBN: 978-1-60604-705-7
1. Fiction/Psychological Fiction
2. Poetry
13.11.20

Dad, my hero.

Mom, my robust queen.

My brothers and sisters, all.

Ryan, my fiancé.

Samson,

Delilah,

Madison,

and Liza

THIS BOOK IS DEDICATED TO

TABLE OF CONTENTS

FOREWORD

Sending in the Clowns, a complex memoir, introduces readers to the life inside the mind of one schizophrenic, author Kris Ralston. Opening the doors into herself for others to walk, self-guided, through chambers explicit and seldom revealed, Kris offers an undisguised glimpse of one girl's journey to womanhood, as a hostage of the illness that is schizophrenia. Eloquence, often born of pain, births poignancy on the road to healing.

This collection of her experiences, full of growing pain and heartache, is written with the tenderness and emotional candor that only a survivor of mental illness can. Her ability to reveal through the written word, the obstacles and triumphs of living with this potential debilitating illness, has been both a gift and an obligation.

Sending in the Clowns

explores and celebrates goodness and exposes black holes of "evil," which line the journey through the universe on the way to the other side of the unknown.

What do you see on the other side of this life on earth? Kris Ralston proves that even in the face of pain, fear, and the demons of oneself, there is eternal hope lingering in the fabric of each day and that what you do with that hope shapes your world one minute, one day at a time. Walk with her for a while, rediscover what it means to exist in the now, retrieve the hope that is offered in every tomorrow.

AnnMarie Knappert,
Fellow student of the University of Washington

INTRODUCTION

About

Sending in the Clowns

Sending in the Clowns is about a small girl who grows up into a world of hatred and malice. All around her is a prison of weirdness, of difference, of social makeup and personal rendition. She is scared; she is lost; she is learning to be different. Scared, mutilated emotionally, and lost psychologically, she swims through the seas of opposing personalities that try to keep her afloat, to bring her to justice, to love, the love of romance and true blessing.

Each character plays a different role, and her makeup consists of strengths and weaknesses that play off each other. The disease of schizophrenia normally becomes apparent in one's early twenties but sometimes appears as late as the fifties or more. The main character in this work is an abused child who grows up into this infernal disease, which lands like a whale upon her. Her struggles through the growing process, the illness, the recovery, to learning how to deal with schizophrenia are filtered through this book, woven with the strings of love, the tapestry of faith, and honey drops of hope.

She begins as little Bertha who grows into Carrie, grows stronger to become Heidi, who sprouts into Fiona, and mystifies her cover with Sabrina, a wholesome, ghostlike presence who interfaces with society at a later age. All in all, there is the necessity of working to protect Dot, the pristine princess, who must be preserved at all cost to make it in this world as a child of God.

THROWING TEARS AWAY

For he has seen everything. All that you do counts, so don't give up on yourself. For once, see the future that is claimed for you. Don't give up; the cleaning bill is too high for emotional wreckage, the torment that leaves behind disgraceful litter, suicide, death, disappointment, and loss to see emotional wreckage cleaned up.

The naughty and the nasty, the perplexed, the poignant and beautiful, confuse what is forgiven and what is forgotten. Forget faith, you can forget all. It is a gift, and without it, there is nothing to hang onto during the waste and disgrace of the naughty and the nasty that has come your way. Bring truth to the forefront and examine it. Who wins? Who loses? Where does the struggle cost effort? Through thick and thin, very clean and foundering. Brave in the places where the animals refuse to claim our noses and ever-pondering eyes. Fallen among the dead where effort has been cut loose and one has tumbled from the cliff.

Careful burning the refuse, where does it all go? We're here in this open system of values and physical features. Blaming yourself gets you nowhere, even when you insist on blaming yourself. Admit your faults and your failures. Find forgiveness, then, for it is the softest "f" word that we have. With fondness we favor forgiveness, to friends and fathers, mothers and daughters, brothers and sisters, even the endless ones, those unborn, but not forgotten.

This is it, the long lost feature that quakes in our stomachs, those features long forgotten, such as control of the weather patterns. Only Santa Claus gets the weather right, so he made Rudolph head of his team, the only one who can show us the right way.

We are not of Santa Claus, but his mischief in kissing Mommy by the tree at night…Oh, those poor children who do not understand love. What is love? The treat at the table? Poor, poor children who haven't seen and experienced love.

It's the feeling that dries up all other feelings and leaves us free and careless, harmless and imperfect. Barely feeling sometimes because it hurts so badly and you don't want to give up too easily.

There is room for practice in the restroom. Practice is fine, sitting there on the toilet as your tears and frustrations melt away in agony, hiding, shamed and unable to believe in the self. Where do your condoms go after you throw them away? A wastebasket, I would hope. Sometimes it's a waste. Why throw away condom after condom, when we could be having babies and babies all over the world? Well, did God give us uncontrollable appetites? Or perhaps we just like the feelings of the soft and fondling natural world. Don't touch or throw away its indignity. Carefully remember that every baby is a life, and too many will trample all of us with resources on this earth.

Meet silly Bertha who didn't know what to do with herself. Hiding behind a name of her own creation, Bertha cried tears every night, for the frustration in her soul brought shame, bravery, and courtship. A new way to be. Flamboyant, sexy, out of control. Bertha learned about condoms soon enough. Babies weren't the right populace at the right time. Some come so unexpectedly.

The right time is the right time, it is also thought, for all babies. Wakened into this world, babies are aware that pain comes with the very first breath. We need each other, the people of this world, different races, sexes, and beliefs. Only by example can we ascertain innocence.

All people are born here with a mission, an intent, and a clear goal that unfolds as days and minutes pass by. Whether conceived in love or by hate, a child's life is not determined but by the seeds that have sewn it. God made all with forgiveness, and even the devil can be forgiven, so there is no excuse to blame a bad life on a bad birth. A bad upbringing is a different story. Bad experiences send molds and dents into our characters. It is our duty to formulate the good in ourselves to overcome the bad.

Poor Bertha, born to have long, stringy blonde hair, was a modest goose chase to herself. She threw her own beliefs, the beliefs of others, and kaleidoscopic significance to fancy for herself a new world, where she could pretend to be real. Not often was her smile unforced, too wide, or melting. Glaucoma surrounded her being, and glasses were forced to comprehend the enigma of life, growing up.

Superfluous were the tears in her eyes, all part of the cryptic costume.

One condom, smashed head, and eyes rolled back. Awakening in the fog of a smelly bedroom, trashed with unsatisfactory papers and partially finished reading books. She was so beautiful, and no one could understand her. Not even Bertha. She couldn't even understand herself, and she never, never knew why. It was only death she hated, one she could not control and must constantly escape. This was her ongoing fear. Self-protection was always imminent.

Believing in herself was one of the most difficult lessons that she ever learned, and it took many nerves, many veins, and hideous, trashed costumes of partially hormone-tainted nuances. Little butt shakes and flaunting of wavy blonde hair. She was suicidal in her manner, constantly laughing herself into the corner of loneliness and ridicule.

She was suicidal of sort but could not reach that conclusion because of something she had once seen. Something in the eyes of her parents as they looked at each other. Something so foggy, steamy, and pure. An erotic feeling passes through her, a look of that famous word, love. Love. She'd seen it more than once, in other eyes as well. She wanted it. She wanted romantic love more than anything, and that consumed her life.

Her poor little life, smitten with rejection and being put on hold. The magic of circumstances never left her resolve, for there was meaning in everything she saw. That was Bertha, Bertha the watcher. She watched everything around her, manipulating with her mind what she could not show in public. Shyness so extreme that her hidden personality could not be found in the maze of excuses and stories she made up for herself.

It was like watching TV, because she did not participate unless she was forced to, and then the action was a creative supposition of what was hidden within. It was a computer without clock. Time didn't matter, even in the event of school, play, or fortitude.

Careful of the watchful attitudes around her, she practiced the art of fading into walls unseen and finding open doorways to slip through before being noticed and gone.

The runaway pattern turned out to be a challenge that wrote stories and stories in her mind. Soon Bertha would graduate to the eighth grade and suffer through more hours of stress and dislike. The classes, so easy. So much stuff so easy if you just tried. There was that little girl in her that demanded good grades. Not everyone has that Nobel Prize hanging over the head. Deadhead, where butterflies turn to nasty moths, and the trail below you turns to quicksand in murky waters.

Beginning again, forging through hour after hour, hidden in a little crevice of her mind, little Bertha swooned in her imagination, letting it take her through life. It was little, she was big. So much to grow into. But not for long, for as the years and hours and minutes walked by, she sat there by the wayside, watching, watching, creating devil after devil in her mind.

Each devil whistled a tune, calling, calling to her human nature, to let the flesh be freed, and forcing it to be flaunted freely in a fashion not fit for the law of God; love and be loved.

Where do we go when the time comes to commit to the truth, and time ticks away the clock of reality, and then you realize it is all real, just different? No one is the same as her, as Bertha, who hides in her greedy kitchen seeking snacks and affairs of the mind with books to catch her fancy. Books don't hurt the flesh. People do. They come up from behind and rape you when you are busy flaunting your flesh for fashion.

It's a sad, sad story, learning firsthand the meaning of rape. It hurts, shames, squashes pride and self-esteem. Confidence disappears into a small bottle in the back of your mind, and then you begin to lie and to badger. Harm them before they harm you. A constant battle, a struggle that needn't be if there is an ounce of understanding in the matter. But what if nobody understands?

Tears come in ounces if you bottle them. They carry us on wings over the harsh reality that must be expressed at last. There are little things and big things that we can do about those tears. Let them come. Let them flow, and then, the big step, share them with a person whom you love and loves you. Man, it feels blatantly small to compare a wretch with disease and a happy college graduate.

A SMALL MOUTH

Curious creatures crawling all over my body, thinks Bertha as she watches ants crawling up and down her skin. The nice soft towel she has laid in the sand on this warm, sunny day is a bed for tired skin, skin wrinkled with thought. Self-affliction as she sucks and chews on her shoulders. Anything to get out the hatred.

Bouncing on the water with an inner tube, she giggles as she peers through the middle of the tube and sees sea creatures sedentary, swimming, and flotsam. She is erotically aroused. There is something about the seashore so entwined with the history of our maker and his made. Evolution is obviously occurring in our bumpy world, and shaking as the world shakes, we see little videos that bring back tears and giggles and picking the nose.

Beautiful trees against

a cobalt summer sky, not a cloud in sight keep waving as gentle north winds come flowing over the beach in the woods.

Leaves blow gently in the wind, and wave patterns, that can be read and understood, if you see, if you let them be watched by your self-afflicted mortality. Monotony is just not possible in the world of God's beauty. The little shore crabs and croaking bullheads under rocks when the tide is out.

Fields of laughing crickets tickle our noses as allergies imbed themselves deep into our lungs and sinuses. Beautiful green fields and climbing hills just doused with sugar-like snow on the upper most branches and rocky ledges.

Smoky beach fires keep shivering to a minimum, as salty skin fights back sunburn and tickles and stings here and there. Squeaky eyes squint with tight wrinkles around each orifice. Protective eyelashes laced with salt bring smiles as happiness is experienced. Just once or twice to let go and crawl out of Bertha's mule cave.

Proud of the plodding feet coming out of darkness, they are brave and useful for making the toughest parts of life slide by...not without personal pain or damage.

Careful attack on the lowliest of life, there is ignorance on the part of butane bottles or vials of considerably diseased blood. Dark and red, full of self-eating germs. Fight back and the answer is starvation, even in the darkness of evening or the recurrence of morning after morning.

Barely proud are the lovers who mournfully lose each other, and the pavement hurts when you fall flat upon it, dumped once again. Pulling out your hair, you reason that there must be something innately wrong with yourself. Barely there sometimes, you are hiding in your shell, practicing words and imitating ideas to develop them further.

Proud is the tail of the spaniel swaying vigorously back and forth and tongue hanging out. Even in the lowest moments, the comfort of a pet relies on the instances we have of declared depression. Mortification as realization of reality kicks in, and the pretty picture of life ahead is not so pretty at all. Not so pretty at all. Kick in to the revving motion of premature living comes into play with thousands of joys and pleasures to be had so small we take them for granted. Picking up the pieces of yesterday is a Newfoundland on a walk with its owner. Dogs are joyous; sometimes they are our only friends. Loneliness is the deepest factor of life, for only one can slip as deeply as the water well goes, not two, three, or four.

The hard part then is to ask for help in coming back up. And our small mouths are sometimes filled with silence because, how do you ask for help if everybody hates you? Who can you turn to that will not betray you or leave you behind in a pile of tears?

Poor Bertha cried every night after her cryptic journey to school. She blanketed herself and crept deeply into the corner of her bedroom wall. *Just disappear,* she thought. *If only I could just disappear. Or what if I expose myself, and someone socks me in the jaw?*

I'm not lethal. I'm not normal. I don't do drugs, and alcohol is only my friend when I can't hide hard enough and I need the nerve to make a fool out of myself. These little thoughts are large manners, and Bertha's gigantic crush on Cliff is no easy matter. Bertha blushes whenever Cliff walks by, and she thinks about him often, staring after his retreating form as he disappears onto a school bus.

Very carefully she hides herself. Maybe he will never know her name, but she will never forget him. Cliff is like many men in her life. Nonexistent. They all have better, more fun things to do. Who plays with Bertha? The ants and other little bugs that crawl around her feet as she eats her well-prepared school lunch every day. Bertha's subconscious tries to think of tricky ways she can socially hurt herself by pretending to be cool and then losing her footing. It is forced social interaction.

Anything to develop pain to the point of self-pity, rejection, and denial. Painful presentation of self and photographs that capture beauty that is beyond beauty. Bertha on the outside is silent and unequivocally gorgeous, just a bit too quiet, so people don't understand.

At least Bertha understands her homework, so homework becomes her best friend. School, learning, and smiling here and there, a little grimace with a giggle. A friendly little giggle, because despite all her pain, which she expertly keeps under cover, there is still a little girl in there trying to be noticed and loved. Bertha is "nice," too nice to get to know. She would rather hit herself over the head with a frying pan, anything to reduce her onward, inward struggle.

It feels good to feel good, and so there are things she likes to do, alone. Reading books is at the top of her list of thing to do and enjoy. Then, pleasurable sensations like tanning in the summer sun or swimming on a hot day. Bertha likes the outdoors. She really is "cool," but that asset has long been taken away from her. Basically, Bertha remains a misunderstood nerd. And so she feels like all nerds, self-absorbed, an extremely late bloomer, and tragic loneliness that must be hidden if coolness is to be captured and maintained as a cover surrounding her being.

Tabatha is a girl that Bertha knows. She is not a very happy girl, and Bertha likes to sit next to her in the classroom. They whisper little but mostly do their work quietly as the rest of the class talks on. Bertha has always been "a pleasure to have in class," probably because of her high test scores and the way she intently focuses on the teacher to understand what is being taught. Bertha can ask questions, but mostly she tries to figure things out on her own. She and Tabatha help each other out of ruts, misunderstanding, and confusion. Tabatha is her friend at school, but no one is her friend out of school. Not even Tabatha wants to be seen with this gorgeously gifted, cryptic problem of preposterous knowledge. Hard work, hard work on that homework, and loved by Mom and Dad, who are mostly interested in her grades and don't really understand her reclusive behavior.

Bertha was hurt, horribly hurt on a business trip that Daddy brought her on, so she would see more of the world, to open her eyes to the differences in culture, to be negligently left alone in a hotel room, where hotel staff found the pretty little thing and had their ways with it.

Bertha calls herself it to disassociate with the childhood molestation that so scarred her for life.

Breathing heavily into her pillow, Bertha tries to erase the experience. No one could possibly have nakedly pierced her with things as her closed eyes screamed with pain, mouth muffled, in darkness she slipped into the wall to watch what was happening. Then came the bathtub, red with her bleeding. Blackness all around, it became a hideous experience as nausea swooned through that body, that body down there breathing quietly into the pillow, forgetting, forgetting all that happened. Merciless hotel attendants preyed upon the little blonde American girl.

Enough! Enough! She's had enough…The voices fade away, loud, laughing voices, leaving the damaged goods behind before anyone returns to the room.

Morning sickness is explained as having had something disagreeable to eat. She can no longer hang on. She must fake it. Back at school in the fifth grade, she no longer clicks with her clique. Born again, Bertha tames the wall closing in on her with a false name, a false smile, and a false family story.

Very carefully she tags along after a couple of people every day at lunch. She tags along and forgets to laugh at the right time. She speaks out of turn and walks away before anyone can answer her.

Dismal in the night, little Bertha dreams about being rescued from the attack by wonderful heroes who carry her home and heal all of her afflictions. Over and over the dream recurs, and with it time goes by, telling her to go and experience life. *No matter what it is, you must do something,* she thought, and it hurts, burns, and stings as rejection and self-hatred put up a barrier between helping others and hating them.

She covers her mouth with her mind and lets out little pathetic squeaks of desperation in her incessant giggles at anything, particularly Cliff, who makes her laugh and she doesn't even know him.

CLIMBING UP THE TREES

Imitation became a tool in Bertha's array of tools for talking, acting, and doing…including when to laugh and how to forget to laugh when loneliness sets in and frustrating, vicious feelings of isolation cause her to lose all meanness. If it hurts to do this, don't do it. Sort of like do unto others like they don't do to you. That's the best tool. Just go along with it, and ignore bad feelings, because, Bertha, you have a big heart, she learned.

Do as you see, not as you're told. Then study, and add your own twist to the homework. Homework; school's greatest invention. Homework is a life outside of life. You didn't really do it, but you learned it. The more you learn, the more prepared you are for the phenomenon of life. It lifts you up for a better view of life and adds understanding to the behavior of others, not only in how they do their homework, but actually in what is learned. It is like a railroad tie, holding the tracks together for the train of life to steam by. To add to your vocabulary, your life experience, and the strange realization that other people have their weird things too.

Even as she spoke, Bertha could not talk. It was all for show, and people called her shy, people called her quiet, and that was signed at the bottom of the page with a swish and swirl of a signature. It was expected that Bertha was quiet. She was constantly hurt, humiliated, and embarrassed. Especially when people began to talk about the way she stared solemnly after Cliff. He knew. Everybody knew. Bertha was miserable, so she changed her name.

She hung from the Cliff of reality, legs like dandelions in the wind, her skirt short and everybody could see it, the painfully abused part. She salted her head and shook it in the wind. Little birds painfully pecked at her forehead. This was where the battlefront began. The front of her head. It disappeared into nothingness, and nobody knew why. Bertha could not take the heat, the spread legs, and the rope hanging from Cliff, threatened to shred away, dropping her into darkness where all evil lives.

Carrie, a funky clown, needed to enter the circus of life next. This was Bertha's funeral, leaving her behind, dead and gone, a back door circus freak, an imitation angel, and a lover of sexy behinds. Dragging behind, she would again resurface, for once a clown, always a clown, and although not aforementioned, Bertha is a clown's personality. Happy, sad, and happy again, altogether, all at once, all the time.

Carrie swore on the truth that there could be nothing better than life. Which life, she did not know. Carefully, she bound her hand in knots with the rope attached to the Cliff of her life, and she swung there in the breeze, barely visible, but hanging on to Cliff.

Grapes and cheese, built to please, Carrie was the yes, yes, yes girl who said yes to everything, hoping to make people like her better. She had no life, she was her life, and all her pictures on the walls of her bedroom were cute little puppies and kittens and one horse. She grew slowly from Bertha the terrified to Carrie, who saw religion and riches. The growing process was nearly impossible. Bertha was practically mute, and Carrie knew she needed to be strong for Bertha in order to fulfill her purpose in life, to find that one true romantic love, despite all adversity. The love she had seen in her parents' eyes. Animals were her escape kingdom. Friends who didn't hurt, backlash, or betray her. Carrie plodded through each day, learning to communicate, to work, and also to discover her body.

Development was hard enough, but even in the blues of matrimony, where she dove for safety in her wishful thinking, she knew that Curtis this and Curtis that was not for her, because Cliff followed her everywhere in her mind, even to bed at night, and especially when she was getting sexy in the shower.

Cliff could draw anything over her in a dream. Curtis was the template of a lousy lover, sticking his big, thwacking tongue into her mouth and panting heavily.

This happened more than once. Bertha detested the type of relationship that Carrie made in search of love. She went to movies, dinners, and high school parties. No fun, time to run. And she did. She was good at rejection, especially for her own protection of privacy when things got too close.

Space was important to her. Bertha needed thinking area, especially when Carrie came knocking on her door. Bertha conceded to self-rejection. Not even Carrie could pry into Curtis without needing to turn around and flee. She cried over loss, even when the loss was for her own inherent safety. Too much exposure and her secrets would be told. Not even her need for love should be known.

Passion came second. It flowed and fluctuated the passive self that wanted to sit down and stare at a wall, with deep penetrating eyes, as her mind grew steadily in strength and fortitude. More ways of lying and pretending. Making up stories and occasionally being honest about an aspect of life, such as the true beauty of a sunrise over the water.

In times of deep reflection it was best to hide in a coffee cup and let the flavor soothe as its character, brown and steamy, mature and molten, liquid and tasty lit up her brain as only a Heidi could enjoy, and did, and so welcomed Heidi Clown into the cast of her life, the clowns of her personality, and the makers of water colors who could abstractly paint her life but never did try.

Red paintings of bloody fingertips were all that she left on the shower walls, silently raging into a ferocious scream, muffled by the terror of being found out. So it just became a burden, and Heidi learned to swim. She swam fast, to impress Cliff, and the other girls were pretty nice to her. Then there was rowing, and that really created a rapturous focal point to her life. Something she could enjoy and imitate, since imitation in each boat was what made it the faster and smoother as one behind another, a crew team could not only race but win blue ribbons as well.

Like a cat in the dark, she could see danger coming before her, but she had not the instinct to run away, retreat, or sufficiently hide. It was almost as if Heidi wanted to get hurt again and again. In a pitiful manner. Pain was her name for a while during the period of her life when she had no other name to explain herself. She shook with disease, the mounting swarm of hornets in her head, and confusion brought Larry into her life, and he only wanted to help her. Amazingly enough, he was able to help. He didn't put a big, swollen tongue in her mouth but gave her little kisses on the cheeks and forehead, and occasionally a flirtatious fling with her mouth, which, believe it or not, she enjoyed.

Larry liked to talk things out, lay down outside at night and carry on with the stars and the moon. It was fun to point out satellites and stars that shot across the sky. She tripped out on Larry, because conversation was not only her weakness but also her downfall. In her weakness she might jump up and turn around in circles, laughing giddily and screaming at the sky. Waving her arms and then hitting Larry, who would get up and move away to talk to someone else.

Very perilous was the walk of life she had on a tightrope. She cried and cried and cried, and Heidi hugged Bertha, leaving Carrie to pretend that everything was okay. Hiding in trees and behind bushes, Carrie got the satisfaction that no one knew where she was. So, slow and silent, Carrie would cry soft tears as she hummed to herself and she played with sticks on the ground.

TIME CLOSING DOWN

Carrie was immature, but nobody knew it because of her cryptic nature. People thought she was weird, or so she believed. To this day she cannot prove that one way or another. She was just extra "shy," and no one really knew her. She was uncomfortable alone among others. She had a gift for making people laugh, sometimes at her own expense; they just didn't care. Peter was just another thought in her head, and so was Derek, just another Curtis. Sabrina Clown arose next at the call of duty. She had the hidden glow, the feminine wiles that led men on to the point of no return. Then she dumped them due to her extreme anxiety about getting to be truly known by anyone. She, the disgusting beauty, drew more attention to herself than she liked, for she shattered under the presence of social attention. Very painful, the experience, and then Hera, the fake, came in to pretend that it wasn't her fault, and then she would find the one person she could sit next to without feeling ashamed. Hera was gone because she didn't work. The meaning of life is work, and if curling hair and putting on pretty makeup is work, than hail to Hera; but if it is cover-up…no good as a slate in the mind of Dot, the main beauty you will meet soon. The meat grinder chewed up Hera, and she wasn't allowed by the faith of Heidi, Carrie, and little Bertha to return to the clown box surrounding Dot.

Hera had a tender fling with Curtis, who cut her down and left her feeling embarrassed about him. It was her "beyond beauty" physical appearance that drew the mosquito men toward her. They swarmed about her, and then they found her out. The box would not open, the box enclosing her true identity, Dorothy, or Dot, as her parents and siblings knew her to be. Everyone saw glimpses of Dot every now and then, and she was so alluring with beauty. The occasionally brutal truth spit out, and a keen insight into the intellect, imagination, and intelligence peeped out here and there, even when Bertha was cradling her punctured groin, leaving her with mistrust of the very truth from which she ran. Something she couldn't think about.

It was painful to repeat over and over again those torturous feelings emanating from her young rape. Belligerent fools. It was enough to swear them out of the Bible and tend them with sincerity to the front of the line where waiting could bring out sweat, dizziness, and yes, mental illnesses.

Failure to freeze in the cold, taking time in maturity with Peter became very loving and sincere, since Heidi had realized that those happy little butterfly feelings swimming in her crotch were lit aflame when she was with him. Letting loose, Heidi met Peter, who was the sort of find that would sit and listen and laugh and occasionally become confused as she became adamant about keeping Dot secluded. Mashed potato in the face. Even Peter knew there was something more, but mostly he tended to those physical yearnings and flowery feelings of physical emotion, affection always cut short by Carrie, who didn't want Dot to live on physical pleasure.

She became the athletic type who practiced again and again, mind over matter. Muscles dilapidated over time as the horrific mental illness crawled, slithering out of the box, leaving Dot confused and shuffling around and wondering about what had happened to Cliff. Just the thought of his name brought her peace, even though she never saw him anymore.

Fast paced and alive, Derek pushed Sabrina over the edge, breaking her rib bone and twisting her arm until it popped out of its socket. Very slowly and reclusively, she sang to herself over and over again, eyeballing Derek over and over, allowing him into her life because he pleased her by putting her down and laughing as she slowly spread her legs for him again and again. Where was her mind? Books. Bertha read every book she could get her hands on. There was a time when reading was a curiosity. Now it was a passion, and poor little Bertha was able to read between the lines, as Carrie, Heidi, and books became best friends. Sabrina, to her credit, read the Bible from front to back and became an avid, practicing Christian. Here she found some solace and became a confirmed catholic, having recently taken first communion and a blueprint about how she should live her life. Here is where true healing began, years ago when a campus missionary placed an NIV Bible in her hands at the University of Washington.

Continually confused about life, Sabrina inherited her awful mental illness from the situations of her life, her birth, and her history. Carrie graduated from high school as the senior class valedictorian, a 4.0 GPA student. She didn't know if she learned everything, and perhaps, as Fiona, she just learned to get by.

Fiona Clown didn't have the medical know-how to heal herself from the onslaught of her mental illness, paranoid schizophrenia. Something happened, something went wrong. No more Curtis to play with her hair and give her back rubs. Poor Sabrina fell over Cliff, and that little infatuation that had kept her so rapt to the truth of a feeling she never did feel again. It was too innocent. Before the loss of innocence in the hotel room.

Bertha was swamped by the reality of adult life and did not allow for crying at every little cut and scrape. Running to Mommy had been her defense for a long time. Now they were friends, and Sabrina stepped aside every now and then so that Mommy could spend short periods of time with her precious Dot. It was Dot who was beyond beauty. Even in the throes of mental illness that the whole family had to deal with, an awesome splendor of beauty shaded the ugliness that this illness manifested in itself.

So, growing up was a feat in itself, and Bertha remained, her lightest defense monitor ready to tell the truth, to converse, to like other people, and to really enjoy herself. It was Bertha who wrote all of Dot's diaries, the ones that got stolen and were read by the general public, much to Dot's demise.

Like her disease, Dot made quite a grand entrance when she was wrestled to the hospital floor, begging these creeps not to cut off her foot, so determined as to scream that she wouldn't die, and she would prove that fact.

THE GREAT DISPLAY

The greatest truth was that Carrie could not shake hands with Fiona. They were monsters to each other. One a hand and foot, the other a sexy abdomen. Carrie felt that Curtis took the best care of her. It was a sneak peek life for Gloria, the prostitute, who made Fiona a maddening excuse for Curtis. He rejected the excuse; he rejected Bertha, the greatest sin of all. Fiona could save all, and she did. She knew that Gloria was a pitiful wretch and isolated her permanently from Dot's suit of characters. Fiona burned Gloria in the trash bin and watched as tendrils of erotic flame slowly disappeared into the sky.

Bertha was the great truth, the great beginning to lead the pack up to Dot, who shone so silly that her attractiveness was a doll's sweet smile and gentle laugh. Not a word. Words, she had long ago learned, could really get you into trouble. Especially written words, like diaries exposed to the public. It was a once-upon-a-time incident where she gained knowledge of herself by this writing exercise. She excused herself very carefully and brought a load of guilt to Curtis, who refused her and gave her as a gift to Derek. Derek the dum-dum. He was cute, he was nice and had a lot of knowledge, but he didn't have the heart she looked for, the pass she wanted to get her into kindergarten adulthood, a relearning of manners and grown-up policies.

Crippled by faith and regurgitating stomach problems known as irritable bowel syndrome, Fiona cried in pain once too many times. She learned the meaning of pure loneliness and isolating behavior. This time Fiona learned and rejected life. Life itself, that even in the throes of the dishwasher, the plumber who raped her, and the kitchen table was always set with decorous splendor. A sneaky time to hide away and drink coffee, consume tea, and read and read and write and write…in this place considered a mansion to poorer folk. It was a house she loved, and Bertha grew up there. She talked to Mommy and played with Daddy, Daddy's little girl and Mommy's special, quiet one.

Larry spanked Mommy once, when Sabrina was imitating adulthood, and he threw rocks at her. They hit, and they hurt. Luckily none hit her in the head, only her knees and ribs. Fat, fat ribs, swelling in the anemia of disorders, causing her to have an eating disorder unrecognized, until it went out of control at Stanford

39

University, where mercilessly Larry lied and comforted her with greasy palms.

That was where her brains blew out. This schizophrenia thing started away from home, on a very lively campus of brainy college students who knew how to socialize. Very confusing, all these strange faces who talked to each other, and none talked to her. *What's wrong with me?* she screamed inside. Even little Heidi tried to fake it, to pretend to be social, and this was analytically painful, since she got nowhere and people thought she was weird; sexy Fiona hanging around the guys, Heidi losing all touch with women except for a couple of black women she found she could talk to and be comfortable with.

Sabrina had a beautiful roommate who prayed a lot, had pictures of Jesus on her wall, and a giant portrait of the Beatles.

THE SOFT HEART

Eunuchs did not much abide at Stanford where Bertha lived in her own little world, slowly pruning Dot, the beauty, into a wretched slut, sleeping here, sleeping there, drinking this and drinking that. Lots of drinking, closet drinking to hide and cover it all up. Fiona tried to smoke pot but had such a horrible reaction that she would never do it again.

Homework just didn't get done. Classes were forgotten, and Carrie went for nice, long, sunny bike rides around the campus perimeter, racing down hills, leaving troubles behind that always reappeared in the dorm again, especially the frightening cafeteria. Even Carrie had to get up and exit the cafeteria through the radio in the kitchen, and this slowly lulled the voices around her into a buzzing noise that left her alone, eating and saying little things, stupid things.

Mulling about in her dorm room, Heidi, the most popular high school student, put posters on her walls and organized her half of the room. This being the first year at Stanford University, accumulating to an exit during spring quarter of her second year. That was fat and lousy. The eating disorder was raging, especially after being diagnosed and put on horrendous anti-psychotic pills. Does this sound heavy for a simple college student? It was beyond her ability to bear. She went home with Daddy and into an array of ignorance, stout approval, and the fat door opened. Carrie cried and cried and cried. Fiona screamed and drank beers. Sabrina sat in her room playing the radio game with her remote control apparatus. This game subsisted of "radio surfing" from song to song to song for hours and hours and hours, and then more hours. Her brain surged with chemicals moving into place that dulled her senses and flattened her feelings and attitudes. She stopped caring. She tripped over her own shoes. She walked at the lake with her Walkman snug around her ears. Music was her greatest therapy, and Curtis, lost long ago, way past the loss of Cliff, became the center of her attention.

Mute and stupid, she clung to him like a retarded dog. An animal out of fresh attention, needing to lick the hand of a trespassing bystander. Her brains, immoral and softly flattering. Licking at paws and sniffing at tea bags. Fiona became like the dog who was her only companion, who also suffered a large eating disorder and attention deficit problem. The two where inseparable. Dog and little Dot, not born yet in full potential. It became writing time. Time to get the words out on the table, to justify faith and begin attending a student Christian group on Friday nights. Another place to feel lonely around people, isolated and rejected too. Except for Christ Jesus through whom she got to know isolation in the midst of godly love and spontaneous laughter. Sometimes she was miserable but not always.

Spontaneous laughter was poisonous. Once upon a time there was a happy girl, and all in all she knew no world of love, life, and happiness, except at a very young age. She softly matured through molestation and rapes, evil insidious conditions for any female being. Likewise, her knowing Cliff was gone, and she had little hope of true love ever coming her way.

She flattered others and laughed at their jokes. Sabrina gradually grew to know how to fit in, even if it was for just a little bit. She cried and screamed and clawed at the walls in the shower. She screamed during the day when no one was home, holding a beer in one hand, and chanting destructive measures for the evil that seemed to follow her everywhere she went. It was conclusive, and it was destructive, except when the music was too loud. Then it became embarrassing, especially when company visited. During these moments she hid herself in her bedroom, Sabrina softly comforting Heidi, who could no longer relate to her pretty self. She was fat, ugly, icky.

She learned a little bit how to play classical guitar and became noteworthy of one tune she liked that was in the beginner's handbook. Believe it or not, Fiona was able to hook a man to take to her. That was not a mistake or a good incident. It simply was. This teacher, this teacher that taught her guitar became her person of significant other. They ate together, laughed together, and Fiona found Sabrina, who was encouraging Heidi to remember social values she had learned in high school.

Dot-Sabrina-Fiona-Heidi-Carrie-Bertha suffer from arrested development. This is a condition in which social development is halted in a retarded manner, due to halted exposure at the right time, and the outlook is weak and enchanting at the same time. Growth does not continue, but watching does. Development equals retardation, which the clowns desperately try to cover up. Growing up socially becomes a personal endeavor, a pursuit of pain.

To begin the process, Dot knew she must attack the entire condition. Super Dot stormed on out. Quiet and frustrating, she sat in corners of coffee shops and read books and wrote in her journal, her constant companion. Eddie, the guitar instructor, became her lover and constant companion. Soon she moved into his house and learned to live with another.

Poor Eddie didn't last long with her. She had a crackup and all fell to pieces, even with the bit of social education that had come with knowing him and being his partner to a large variety of musical social events. After initial agony and embarrassment, she learned how to hide and be social at the same time. She smiled a lot; things weren't quite so embarrassing anymore.

Chewed-up college information made her an

interesting conversationalist, but only when Sabrina let Fiona lead the way.

She made the mistake and tried to be Fiona, as Heidi was burdened with the weight of a struggling midsection and parallel focus. Very important, because of years in arrested development, Fiona lived as a cryptic statue, beautiful and obviously important, but no one knew why.

As far as some people knew, Sabrina, inhabited with Heidi, in composition was an attractive person that was impossible to get to know, and she was brushed off as having "nothing there" as far as personality. Even in the darkest of times, she was unable to open up, for the danger of Bertha being identified was furiously frightening.

She flew like feathers on the wing, mostly in her car. Driving gave her good time to think with changing scenery, so she wouldn't find herself dwelling and suffering at the same time. Sometimes she would try to volunteer or work somewhere, but after two months or so, there was always a break. Sabrina couldn't stay employed. She was mature, wise, and smart to others, but to herself, Sabrina remained a failure. If it wasn't for Heidi, her arrested development would never have had an impetus to launch her across the deep chasm of social illness into the world of reality as a person.

Larry came around to bother her every now and then. He became a problem to her, and she didn't know what to do. She was isolated, meaningless, a pretty little sex bag. Some people were just too much. For a fine young innocent thing that Fiona was, there was always someone who stared too much, bothered her with flirtatious gestures, and Fiona wanted to throw up in their faces. It was better to face her illness than get too ill too many times. These were the personal times, the hidden screams, the lonely outpour of prayers.

There were pregnancy scares, but never anything but false alarms. The best times were reading. Sabrina liked words a lot. They were her expression. In therapy she learned to identify with Dot. The game was to get Dot to take in Bertha, so that the true natural beauty could appear, flaunted by Fiona, described by Heidi, and reinforced by Carrie.

Sabrina would disappear once pretending was no longer necessary. Sabrina would leave, leaving behind a bold ability to act, fake, dodge, hide, brag, hit, and growl. Little devices here and there to help smooth a desperate road. Lugging along a frozen condition that needed to thaw. This was schizophrenia, the need to make up, the ability to make up. Make up for self, for loss, and for gain. The need to walk backwards in a forward situation. The ability to sit on a pin without screaming. The need to take pills in order to prevent hideous psychosis so awful that Sabrina's sister called her ugly, and that's exactly what she was in the end, before backing out of the arena, going in enormous strides to the place where she could see herself as a real person.

Immune to gain, Sabrina saw herself as being flat. Boring, idiotic, and void of thinking. She was fake, false, endearing to evil, and beginning as an addict to faith...a pure faith that addicted her in a paralyzing way, where the higher power in her life manifested itself and became a constant need and urgency to stay inside of her, expressed through prayers and Bible study. Soon this "addiction" settled down and became known to her as love. Fiona screamed, Carrie rolled over and over like a dog in glee, and Bertha smiled a little bit to know the love of God.

God loved us before we knew him, before we could love him back. That's where Sabrina began to fade, a ghost leaving the body, in dead silence. Fiona lost herself and was filled instead with a personhood known as her spirit, missing since the destruction of Bertha long ago in the fifth grade, in the hotel, in the hot, sunny country of Singapore. Ugliness turned to despair, where chilling sensations became automatic and fruitful with every new positive motion in her life. Books were still her friends. Fiona grew and grew; building parameters of landscape all about her, developing personality after the arrested development had been bridged.

Heidi hid in deep agony, feeling the depths of her pain broken off by life-changing events that pulled the rug right out from under her. Her painful hose were too tight, and the tiger was constantly at her back, threatening, threatening. She paralyzed herself with anger as the years went by. Irritable bowel syndrome became a horribly annoying issue. So much so that Carrie took her riding in the little blue car that Daddy had provided for her, practicing stopping at gas stations to go to the bathroom. It was a dangerous fear, walking around and never knowing when the flow would become too insistent.

Freezing in corners of the library, she labored on

shelving books in her mind, taking the good, and leaving the bad. Words meant more to her than anything. Carrie learned that words could get you in and out of situations, although Heidi occasionally stomped on her with jealousy and anger, that anyone should survive a panic attack and live, with the will to live…it was unfair. There was never any relief for Heidi, the guru who liked to plan lives and fix lives, anything to discredit herself from validity in life.

Excuse her, but she did not believe in herself, even the self she had lost. An ignoramus in full-fledged anger. Vicious sexual experiences consumed her from the inside out, causing her to hide and flare up, punishing, pushing on self-destruction to the ultimate cause of insulting her spirit. And this became lethal. Although Heidi never succeeded in killing herself, she tried once, but stopped when hope stepped in around the corner. Some certain song, she didn't remember what it was, Heidi saw hope and wrapped herself up in a robe of deceit.

She saw things. She saw faces in the cement when she walked along. She saw Jesus walk her home one rainy day after being off her medication for four days and nights. Jesus led her directly to her medicine cabinet and then disappeared. Call it true or false, the explanation was clear to her. Take those infernal pills and live a little better, just a little bit better.

Carrie played with the dog a lot; although he didn't know how to fetch, he made a good wrestling partner. Never bit her and liked going for walks. Carrie would disappear, however, when Fiona saw Heidi take an unmerciful, long look at a guy wrapped in trousers and a nice T-shirt. This guy was an imprint for a lot of guys. Fiona hated them, and Heidi teased them in her mind, planning weddings ahead of times for a man whose name she did not know.

Planning things was part of her life. Planning how to make it through the day, how to make the most of the day, and how to get married without knowing anyone to marry. Marry, marry, marry. It seemed to be the only answer, the love, the spark, the harmony that she witnessed between Mom and Dad.

Growing up was difficult; it had so many faculties. There was the danger factor of getting run over in the street. There was the confusing factor of having too many choices. There was the medium factor of not angering other people, living a diplomatic way of life. There was marrying the man who wasn't there, the ghost of her dreams. Fiona began to sort through these problems, knowing that there was no real solution. This is life, and Heidi has to obey her part, unless Dot should turn out to be a blemished monster.

She gets all the moves, watches all the tunes as winds blow in the trees. The sound of magic is a torment of believing that things will get better soon, hoping that the next day will be a miracle. But it is a miracle that never comes. She overcomes obstacles and makes a personal straightjacket. Heidi needs to cleave herself to the truth. She lost herself at a young age, and her magic now is a twinkle in the eye that everyone seems to like.

It is a burden of the yoke to have to pull your troubles

with you up the mountain. And you need your support system of people, your doctors, therapists, parents, siblings, and friends there in order to sort through problems that mesh with troubles on the way up, providing a stepladder that rises with each step.

Eating porcupines and burning palms on the grill are two extremes of listening and not letting go. It burns like guilt in the kiln, forming self as new self, as spirit and faithful. Let go, let run, then reel it back in. Too many fishes out there. The many in the sea, the one to marry.

Turquoise and brown, a muddy flaw that throws dirt in the face and remains puke on the bed of brown necessity. What a guilty feeling, to know that everyone doesn't hate you, but believing that they do, even in the mighty range of a guitar. Suicide envy, a place to go where mending the broken knee is stranger than putting back together the cracked skull.

Your soap is necessary in the wind in the tunnels of confusion and guilt. Portraying "easy does it" channels the wind gently as you learn to surf the wind on the waters. Float, fly, bounce high and rigorous as the team you lead follows a distant, ignorant monster. The monster is weak and gnarly, tugging at corners to upset tablecloths and minding the manners of the meek by ranging their territory in a set perimeter of discipline. There is the Bible and how to live by it.

Even in the tunes of the circus, the clowns dance and sprawl, some gay and happy, others sad and envious. A smile with a frown, a frown with a frown. That is the reality, other than having two smiles. So, to have more than one clown is necessary.

It is pertinent to the bothersome crystals of life that keep us excused from the ever after. Guilty, punished, and bearing burdens of life and death, leading to new life, and so on. Guilty, the range of guilt deserving punishment, and the range of leaving deftly before anyone notices.

Clear as an angel in the wind, there is the wind dance that we recognize in the trees. It is good to study these wind patterns, a way to free the soul and let it settle again in a new place. A place to pivot, turn, and do something. It's not very good to do nothing, for there is no place for guilt or punishment or justice that might suffice as innocence.

Torrents of rain come down in the back of the brain. The clown smiles and counts out her sides. The side of big sin, dominance, excuse, dexterity, make-believe, sorceress, and princess.

Sad and happy are the two most obvious features in any personality. There is depression, there is glee. Even in the saucy face of Fiona, there is make-believe to say that the next man whose hand you shake you will marry. It doesn't work, no matter who you bump into and introduce yourself to.

There is a danger of falling off the edge, so the sorceress of Sabrina makes books in her mind and several reels of movies all running at the same time. Who could possibly function under these circumstances? Hanging on through a tight string, a bodily squeeze, as Heidi steadies the maneuver of dark to light in the inner sides of heaven.

Each of us can feel heaven; the trick is to recognize it. Even in horrible situations, heaven can be accessed. There is nothing thrilling about a small step of progress. But progress in your life is a touch of heaven. Here you can see it all around you. The Good Samaritan helps the fallen man on the side of the road.

Fall down yourself, and you never know if someone will be there to pick you up. Sometimes you have to do it yourself. Very funny, you agree, because, yes, we've all been there. Some time you need to learn to depend on yourself, even if it is painful.

Pain can prevent. It can also provoke. It is a necessary part of life that teaches how to know what is right and what is wrong. Some hurts are good hurts, and some are satanic, they feel so bad. Whatever the course, there is always room for change, like learning to love the devil, who once was our greatest enemy. Now you are your own greatest enemy, and it depends on guilt and the floorboards that break when you step on them. The insistent trapdoor that gives way at most any time, usually unexpected and devastating.

The nearness of the creatures around you is a precursor to hatred or to love. Some people want to hurt you; others don't care. Still, there are those who want to help and heal you. Half of the battle is knowing your enemy and loving your enemy. It just works.

A guarantee is phenomenal. Who can be so sure that something will come through? Who threw the dart that missed the target? Is the clown tall or short? Short like Bertha, tall and windy like Sabrina, tightly squeezing like

Heidi, breaking away to attract like Fiona, can't forget Carrie, and the princess of all mankind, Dot herself.

Does Dot wear a crown? She does, and laces in her hair too.

She is the tall pine tree that never will break and burns the hardest when limbs are cut off for fire. For pruning.

Max too is a tall pine tree, planted for the purpose of changing bad to good in other people. Max is new, he is old, and he is part of everything. He loves Sabrina; it was love at first sight. Adulthood has arrived, and Sabrina has many skills in the social world, for she has practiced hard and painfully. The putrid, old, and stinky past is the face of the devil, who is truly ugly and knows it. What does he have to do with Max? Max is a tree just like Dot. A tree is perfectly planted in every case. Every human is perfectly made. But some fall for the fire, the flames of envy, curses, and rot. Not Max; his branches are not chaff, thrown to the flames of hell. He dances and sways in the breezes. Branch to branch with Dot, madly in love with Sabrina, who will eventually disappear and give rise to the perfect schizophrenic, clown, princess, Dot.

Bugs are everywhere, and Heidi freezes with terror when there is a bee in the car. She is afraid. From a young age, small Carrie has been petrified of bees after accidentally stepping into a clown's trap, the hornet hive of all hornet hives, that whipped, ate, stung, and pierced her again and again and again; eight times as she ran away the fastest that those little legs could carry her, as Bertha whispered into her ear that everything would be okay.

That was a big breath. A breath-around-the-block

breath. She couldn't escape them, they were everywhere, and they chased her; they followed little Carrie so far she lost sense of safety and fell helpless into Mommy's arms, even as the nasty things pestered her until Mom got out the Raid and stamped the hornets underfoot.

It was an eager presentation. She wanted more but got little. There were very many wasps all over the world; to her misfortune, she happened to step on an old rotted log full of hornets.

Tears were running out of Carrie's eyes as she lay on Mommy's bed to ease her shock and freezing terror. It was not a relaxing afternoon.

EMBARRASSMENT

Cheating in class was not an option. Carrie had values of hard work and determination. She liked to do her own work, she liked to take pride in her work, and she did. Perhaps her antisocial demeanor made her more focused on schoolwork. Curtis was her playmate/boyfriend, if such a relationship could exist at some age, and it did. Curtis turned her off, though, with his sappy ways and slow, desperate attempts to secure her as his own.

Little tips here and there made Carrie all the wiser. She was stronger than Bertha, who could not shoulder her load alone. She found as years went by she grew stronger and a little bit more secure. But Carrie didn't have a friend in the world except for her dog and the books she constantly stuck her nose into. Deliberating on the words, the writing, the fascinating venue of other people's experiences, she blazed her own trail, alone, inward. She shook off compliments she knew were not true. Nobody really knew Carrie, only that she grew around Bertha and lifted her up to the heavens of improvement.

She ate cake and cookies, fattening foods in large amounts, especially after beginning the anti-psychotics she was prescribed at Stanford, when she had "turned herself in" because of the messed-up confusion she was having that was all a lot of pain. Pain, fear, ache, and a wish to die.

Like a big skeleton in the closet, she slowly swayed back and forth to rhythmical noises that passed for music in the room where her bed laid occupied by herself for several hours a day and all night long.

Singing when no one was around seemed like an outlet. For some reason, there had to be an outlet. Finally, Heidi began to see a psychiatrist after returning home from a medical leave of absence from Stanford University. Everybody needs someone to love and be loved. Dirty, dusty conditions clouded everyday experience in her bedroom at home with Mom and Dad, where screaming was allowed during the day, if not understood.

Cleaning became a regular practice. To get the dust, dirt, and soap buildup all around the living room, bathroom, and kitchen. The bedroom was organized daily, including computer for journaling and sending a few e-mail messages back and forth with chosen family members.

The importance of family became paramount. She cried in her sleeve and slobbered in her bed at night.

Books became a necessity. Fiction, spiritual, self-help, and history were top of the list. Everybody learns from books, so why do some people not like reading? It doesn't make sense to me, unless skills are lacking.

Fire and fun don't mix together. Even in the top, high rungs of the city, there is always someone higher somewhere else, until you meet the utmost, God, of whom there is no one higher. Bleak and sincere, our little hearts beat at a pounding measure to keep us alive. Who knows what comes after that? After the heart stops?

Even Heidi wondered what death was like. But scarier than her own death was the death of someone close that she loved. The nearness of clown love, the truth of smiling through depression.

Everybody laughs at Heidi. She can't hide herself well enough to stay insignificant, and when she is discovered, she forgets to act on cue. She gets shaken up in the common thunderstorm and cries out when the pain of harsh emotions becomes too great.

Favorable events can turn around a bad mood at the snap of the fingers. It is daring and inconclusive, the little turn here and there that gets one lost. Figure in the ousted feelings of neglect, refilled by feelings of rejection. It's a combination powerful enough to sink anyone's mood to the level of self-hatred and harsh judgment of others.

Then, if you judge others, you learn to hate them too out of bitterness and jealousy. It's an icky, yucky feeling to feel lost and inconclusive, a spirit hanging around in search of a stable home. Fight for flight, and fly to avoid fighting. Headache twisted around in search of sloppy behavior that remains comfortable to all.

Sometimes Heidi felt like her head was going through a meat grinder. The pain so great that not even a good cry could help, because a good cry was so rare that the only way to deal was with horrible shrieking and misfit action. Hopefully there was success in life. Heidi, reminded by Carrie, would never forget the spark of love she'd seen in her parents' eyes. Something so beautiful. Something to cling to, the idea of love, true, romantic, gentle, safe, and caring love. Love that accepted everything, even disagreement. Even bearing the burden of a silly, old clown like Carrie, who would develop into Heidi, then Fiona, Sabrina, and last and most precious, Dot.

Bertha was not forgotten, but she was never very difficult to deal with. All she knew was that people like Cliff existed in the world. People to be sought after, yet in helpless remission, for Cliff disappeared as Carrie lifted up broken Bertha to bring her to remission.

Crying and dancing at the same time, Carrie handed her beauty to Heidi, that she might find healing in the world of hope around her. Hope, because other people seemed to have it better. Much better. Guilt, jealousy, hatred, and quarrelsome behavior with herself made her stiff as a rock and tough as pepperoni.

There had to be something good about her condition. Unbeknownst to her, Heidi was learning the art of patience. Patience through love, hatred, pain, and suffering. Learning and suffering is the art of patience, even through clowning around that makes you feel silly and worthless at the same time, giving meaning to your life.

Cleaning your junk out of the closet is enough to send anyone on a mental road trip, where you find yourself in the end. Deep waters, moving asunder, lapping at your toes as you hang there helplessly across a broken river bridge. Lost and alone, you yearn for help, but the worst is usually when you are all alone. You fall in as your grip is torn away from you.

The waters are cold and violent. Sending you careening through all aspects of life, where water is necessary, vital, and yet an end to all means, if that is your fate.

Cleaning out the closet causes the river to rise, becoming molten as you are washed ashore against some tree. Fate is exact calculus against necessity. The through and through that winds about eternally until you figure a way out. That was Heidi's greatest dilemma. She could not think and focus at the same time. Her urgency to think and communicate left her naked and cold in places where people could touch her. Molestation, rape.

Sabrina slapped her face. How dare Heidi bare herself that way? As if her body were a tool for men, for men to play with, fondle, and rape. She was guilty in her own mind, and her harm caused ongoing pain that she respected as her own fault.

She lived with it, knowing no other life, unless Bertha's profound memory told her that things really can be innocent, if life is real and worthy of the tools of Christ. Her language was shy and cryptic. No one really knew her. The very fact of negligence was the fault of her own tool, her brain, which troubled her constantly in voices, malicious thoughts, and disobedient behavior, leading her to behavior that was personal and faulty. Just that one time she went out and ordered herself a cognac, but had not the guts to finish it. Conscience lives on; it is not affected. It is like a weather vane. It orients life in patterns of experience. It is fateful and a guiding light.

Like little stars in the sky, there arises a pattern to every person's life. No two are alike. With three you can make comparisons, weighing your options, and delighting in similarities, the beginnings of friendship. Fiona was able to fake it if she stepped all over Heidi.

Heidi gave her sticky feet, a firm foundation where she could act like a clown and hurt and cry while everybody saw her laughing. Crying out could not help; it only worried people too much, the wrong way.

People faked it. They were not truly concerned. The behavior of life is enough to draw upon in fake moments to trade Heidi instantaneously for Fiona, who walked on her, as Sabrina slapped her around a little.

They ganged up on her together. Fiona teased and tormented Heidi, while Sabrina whacked at her every turn of the head. To Sabrina, the sorceress, Heidi was purely evil, and everything she did was wrong.

Heidi, however, was stout as a tree trunk, and no one could push her around, and, luckily, no one had weapons or chain saws to deplete her form and imagination.

Like a big, fat pig in the middle of a marsh, Fiona slipped and slid over Heidi wherever she got flogged by Sabrina, until, finally, she no longer played games with her and began to take her seriously, defending her from Sabrina, learning to live the life of a well-made Christian princess.

Princess? Fiona knew about Bertha, the first defense against annihilation. She was big, and strong, and beautiful. Strong and beautiful and retarded. Little princess…but not while Sabrina was present. She would be a queen if she could, but Fiona knew that the only queen was in heaven. Her life, her *self* was a born princess, living on laughter and joyous occasion.

Sabrina would fly away some day but always would leave an imprint on the life of Dot, the most perfect clown of all.

She riddled Heidi, making her a clown in the face of ice cream fallen from a child's cone to the ground. Behavior was beautiful. It took days and days to make it through one dilemma at a time. Sometimes there was nothing to do. On days like that, there was the companionship of her dog, her Bible, and, believe it or not, her parents, who loved her unconditionally.

Faith played a major role in getting through each day. When Heidi got hit over the head with a frying pan, or, rather, with the onslaught of mental illness, her growth halted, and she began an inward spiral of the self of being, the psyche, the mind, soul, spirit, and heart. She began a self-examination, since there was no other way of coping. Burdensome traction kept her from growing at a natural rate. She was successful at failure again and again and again. Until it became a learning process. A princess in the throes of mental illness is unheard of. Her little-girlie nature kept her from being too far from falling off the suicide cliff. There was always something to hold on to, even if it was the falsehood of her own imagination.

Screaming, screaming, again and again, there are no adequate words for explaining the sort of mental psychological pain that wracked her mind and body every day. The medicines helped minimally, but the pain was relentless.

So she became tough material on the inside, with a very thick skin against outward agitation. Very many people would have liked to walk over her, and many did, so many held grudges of jealousy and revulsion. Some knew her before the Bertha era began, when soap bubbles still held magic. When her wonder mixed with her intelligence, and she hobbled along with a time bomb inside that blew at the end of high school, with a trail of smoke leading up to it.

The time bomb that went with her everywhere and decided when and where it would explode inside of her, totally disabling her mental facilities, her reasoning, and her psychotic innards.

It kept her shut in a lot, and she became afraid of going outside. But her body needed exercise, and mindless as a mummy, she walked with the doggy all around the neighborhood…this was after returning from Stanford, where the nuclear bomb that had been waiting exploded during her second year, following a few smaller hits leading up to that during her first year and last parts of high school. How do you deal with that?

It was an unclean situation, sordid relationships and

broken pride. Falling, falling from valedictorian honor to probation. It was evil, ugly, disgusting, the mutilation of her mind as Sabrina went on trips that made her feel real, even though it was all the more fake. There was always Curtis, who stuck by her side, who wanted flirty Fiona but would never get her because of the mirage she portrayed. In the end it was a hobbling-forward race with Heidi and Sabrina at each other's throats and sending Fiona to hell. Fiona, the only one who could deal, had to be fake about it. They smothered her, vying for attention. Heidi and Sabrina had swords of words and actions that covered Fiona with fallout. Then they ripped at each other's self-expression. Girl or woman? Who was this enigma? This princess. This Heidi, losing the battle morosely, yet knowing that there was nothing but hatred left in the storage of hideous knowledge…the gold at the end of the rainbow. Truthfully, it is so false that there is gold at both ends of the rainbow.

Bracing herself, this mother, Sabrina, must take care of her inner child. So strong and expressive, her tumultuous way of acting with hideous concourse left her in the midst of suicidal depression. It was glee, to be lifted by a cup of coffee, a walk, a few hours in the coffee shop with pen squiggling gaily in her right hand, a book later to take some attention. But so alone…until Curtis. And she shies away in remembrance of this button-down man, whose kaleidoscopic way of entertaining her left her laughing innocently, with a ray of hope for herself in the world where Fiona petted Heidi, and together with the experience of bustling Carrie and pristine, holy Bertha, there was a renewal, and faith grew out of leaves in the lawn. Like weeds on a rainy day, still beautiful.

Very sad and ongoing is this elusive need to remain in contact with each other, the personalities of Dot, who each behave in another manner, in order to be faithful to the preservation of Princess Dot, that all might respect and adore her in the end. It is a broken condition where each part must compromise, and when fights break out, the winner is the conglomerate clown who gains strength from decisions of ownership of power. It is a pristine gathering and a social breakdown. Where running to Mother must become running to the self, for help, even for advice against suicide. For Dot is beautiful and has a lot to live for, once all the clowns get their acts together.

Tender, failing and flailing screams cause shouts of praise from Fiona, who sees the goodness in Heidi, the poor remnant of natural socialization. It's pancake batter in the pan, the way it stretches and bubbles and needs to be flipped. Just like suntanning needs a flip every now and then.

Too much exposure causes burning, and so it is with artificial socialization. One can be only so creative before the truth comes knocking on the door and we no longer understand the separation between the *I* and the *You*. When the knocking gets loud enough, all souls take position for the entry of the Lord. The Lord knows the truth, and there is no other way to find it. Dot is always in search of the truth. But that takes time and is really hard. However, the truth be known, little by little the truth will always come out. As little by little we let it inside of ourselves.

Careful concentration allows everybody to reach the truth inside of themselves, and this is not always a happy experience. Where do I come from? Where do we belong? Who is my master? What watches over me, and why?

Belonging and beholding are different than owning. Justification is the one truth that shines true with everybody, even if it is evil.

Poor Heidi will never move again. She is a stump in the ground with tendrils of beauty spurting out of the ground into her magnificent, circular strength. Like a clasp, she hides within herself all the glory of Dot, Dot at an immature stage, unspoiled and happy.

Wasted like the can she was found in as a tossed-away baby girl. Someone found her squeaking at the bottom of a garbage

HUMILIATION

can. As a baby, an infant. These were parents who cared a lot. Yet, her life was destined for difficulty and madness. For schizophrenia, depression, and anxiety. It was a horrible combination, leading to a treacherous life, like a clownish whore, who laughed during the act of rape and cried during emotional movies. Violent movies made her nauseated, as did her human sexuality class in college. At one point she ran out of the room to avoid vomiting.

Heidi never cried at her high school graduation. In fact, she felt nothing at all and merely went through the motions, having refused to give the valedictorian's speech. Heidi was one to hide, not one who showed off. She was incredibly embarrassed and tried to hide in her seat in the thirteenth row on the right side. She ambled shyly up to the stage and across it, accepting her diploma. How scary to think of college. But according to Dad, there was no other option.

What a waste of time. But, then, is anything really a waste of time? All learning is experience, even losses and failures, for there is no waste of time. Yet who can say? Where is the judge that communicates our performance with our outcome? What have we done with the time we are given? God knows. The meaning of life is work. God spits out the lazy.

If you limp from falling, is that a waste of time? Perhaps time can't be wasted, but life can. Life can be wasted by choosing to do nothing during those off times where schedule lacks calling. Creativity needs expression. Show yourself; don't waste your life. Leave something behind you when you go to the next life. That's not a waste of life.

Red cannot be blue, and blue cannot be red. It is a difference of opinion that makes the world go wrong. Some choose red, some choose blue. Then, there is yellow. Yellow is the most bright, the color of the sun that tans and browns us. Blue is like the sky that hangs the sun, and red the very blood in our vessels. Why think about these colors, because they are traditional instincts. Everybody relates more closely to one than another. There are some things that don't change, and that is a matter of opinion until compromise is reached. When all the ingredients of the batter are mixed together and baked, a cookie is formed.

Baked and formed into something useful to eat. So, when people's opinions are collaborated, there is a new idea formed, and the old becomes new. New opinions that become wholesome ideas and form encouragement to life. That was Carrie's job. She is a little steam engine, keeping the life of Dot running in order for the upkeep and timing of society. She is changing with the times, believing in the faults and behaviors of others.

Calculus and intimacy grow together if taken to the maximum. If Max is perfect, and he is, according to a budding Dot, then there is hope in every sanctuary of crime. People believe in evil, but it is not wrong. It is a state of mind that pulls apart what has been put together sensually and erotically. The son of the female dog who did not do his part in putting life on its course of freedom.

Apt to do things that are impossible, the beginner does not believe in limits. There are limits. There are things that are impossible, such as the lining of the universe. It's way out there, and that's the sort of thing that Heidi, Fiona, and Sabrina think about when they collaborate their thoughts and opinions. They can't get past the limit of impossibility, but they can conceive of it.

As a resolve, there is always the limit of altruistic love, doing good for others, until there is no more to give. Give away, give onward, and build toward a better future. The future is so important to us, because upon it lies our total existence. In the night, during the day, the time goes by and life is lived. Sabrina is fun for people to watch and gives Fiona many ideas to keep from being bored. As a known fact, she never, ever gets bored with secluded Heidi, enraptured Carrie, dancing Sabrina, and the ongoing task of preserving Bertha's innocence as Carrie cries for her.

This multitude of feelings is enough to show off that self-love is important in building up self-love and self-character. Giving together and sharing in love does not implicate the destiny in all of us. That is fear and the rapture of giving up hope to die in the arms of love. Where sweet, sweet patterns of love come falling upon the little ones who cannot carry the loads of an adult. Arrested development can be confusing and look fake. But it isn't fake. A tall, physically developed person with no apparent abnormalities should be able to bear the load of anyone. But consider the mental abilities, well hidden, and such excuses are no longer thought of as so beyond reach. Patterns of love falling down all around us bring success to the failures of yesterday. These are not wasted times. They may hurt, but like the saying goes, "No pain, no gain." Paralyzed in thought, we come to the tomb of all, the place where we say, "I give up." That is not a sin and can be accepted as a valid choice or option, not to think less of the person. Sometimes we're just going in the wrong direction. And we can feel it. Some people should be in special education classes at school, yet their need is not identified.

Some people just fake it, and this was Heidi, who never cheated but always memorized the right answers, not the right ideas. Poor, humiliated Heidi, who could not speak up in class, but she could write her tests and papers, and with some satisfaction.

Hiding Heidi, she became known to herself, although not in such nice words. More like terrible, moron, beauty queen genius. Heidi despised cheating and could tell when people were copying off her paper. She would shuffle her shoulder around to block a sneaky classmate's view of her work.

Lemon head. Impossible to communicate. Is this schizophrenia in its early stages? Withdrawn, wizard, unsocial, self-worry, crying, pain, and broken-hearted loneliness?

Boring, bruised, and broken. Betrayed, beaten, bumped, battered. Better not beat on that broken path. Too many people all around, always. Solitude so precious, until there was no other option. When loneliness took the biggest chunk out of Heidi that ever was used. Broken, as a string hanging from a concrete slab to a concrete slab. Broken and patronized, the thought of clinging to the path is often what keeps us hanging on.

The path is often winding, with crossroads and switchbacks, giving children the chance to grow of their own accord. It is simple to make a decision but often in congruence is difficulty in living by that decision. Each child will go a specified way, no two exactly the same. Spending more time together builds friendship and trust. Not so easy in a world of hate and envy. Competition, comparing oneself with others. Friendship can be hard to come by. Everyone is so afraid of making mistakes or messing up.

Hoarding and pinching, it doesn't matter. People always want more and more, and there is a story about that:

There is a negative shuffler who scuffles about the house, claiming there is nothing to do and nothing to be done. This horrible monster has no hope. There is always something to be done. It just needs doing.

The monster of hope is that people are afraid of it because they doubt themselves and beat themselves up too much. Is it too much to ask? To be afraid and have courage to face any path you have beaten down?

Helpful voices ask for attention. Others hook you while fishing but beg you not to tell. Vociferous patterns of disregard and roasting on the fire while bugs fly triumphantly in the air. They fly in patterns known only to themselves, where no two can be exactly at once. Clowns, clowns, and more clowns. Too many to name, so I will stick to those already mentioned: Bertha, Carrie, Heidi, Fiona, Sabrina, and Dot. Then: Cliff, Curtis, Derek, Larry, and Max.

Captain 91422. Just a random selection of numbers, but he is swiftly enough to come to the rescue after Fiona was raped by Curtis and bullied by Derek, the two having teamed up. Wasps were in an uproar, and Captain 91422 knew exactly what must be done, but the lies were in his favor and justice was not done.

Serving in the court of justice were Master Flower and Sweet Justice Lemon Head. Curtis and Derek got off not guilty. Soon after, Master Flower dried up and wilted, and Sweet Justice went bitter and cold. They disappeared into the atmosphere, carrying their evildoings with them.

Bitter and hated, enemy to all. Their true names? Money and Stock. Who could fight the power of the means of what makes our world go around? If an

BELLIGERENCE

infant is sick, do you watch it die, or do you take it to a doctor who knows how to diagnose and treat the given illness?

If a little girl is raped, can she be healed as well, or is she blamed in the end for something she cannot speak about, a tale too evil to tell? Every evil, every injustice. So Fiona dances on Heidi, who gets burned as though in hell, as Carrie madly follows the road set out by Bertha, and sorceress Sabrina allows the mind of Dot to exit this strange situation to travel in dreams and alcohol where the devil will not bother her, for navigation has been wisely set out by the heavens, and Carry has followed Bertha to strange passes of peace.

Curtis and Derek follow as anonymous characters that do evil things symbiotic to their characters. They act and send and frown and grow and expand and become big, ugly monsters that no one wants to lay eyes on. A glance in the direction of either one is temptation for molestation and worse, enormously unjust acts.

Bouncing up and down, Carrie is carefree as she wiggles around and orients herself today to keep from being idle in case Curtis or Derek walk by. And they will. They always will. By the grace of God, Carrie kicks Bertha to go stand by some other quiet girls in the schoolyard at lunch where she can fit in without talking. Here is respite. No one will bother Dot here; there are too many quiet girls, minding their lunches and tending to homework. The bell rings and it is time to go back inside.

So, she survived another lunch. Back inside it is a

Cliff day. Her eyes follow him all over the place. She walks past her own room just to see where he sits down in woodshop with his cool, cool friends. Carrie cries, and Fiona stumbles over her shoelace as she launches herself back to her own math room, praying he hadn't noticed. Angry Heidi brushes off her jeans as she gets up to go sit in her middle chair in the back. She blushes fiercely, burning in her ears, her eyes boring holes into the math book in her hands.

What a big, bumbling idiot I am, she thinks to herself. She pulls out her homework. She gives it in. She doesn't care. She already knows: A+. She'd figured out each problem.

Focusing on each problem that the teacher put on the board that day helped her confused mind settle down and think clearly, too clearly, as tears followed her thoughts of Cliff. If only she were older or her breasts were bigger. If only she wasn't so shy. If only she wasn't always hiding herself. The matter at hand speaking of the trouble in her heart. What is love? Does anyone love me? How can I make Cliff love me? That is what hurt so bad. She couldn't. If she could just smile at him. But she couldn't. Whenever Sabrina passed Cliff anywhere, she could only manage to flash a frown. *This hurts,* she thought. So she lost Cliff. He fell off her life, and down she fell after him, avoiding sticks and branches. The balloon popped, the baby love disappeared, and Dot began to heal as her love for Cliff began to turn inward to herself.

So she believed that men had some good in themselves somewhere, somewhere that was unknown to her. Her first little relationship that did not backfire came along to her through Larry, a coworker she met at a piano shop. She liked to sit down and play along with him, creating beautiful music that brought customers into the shop. The job didn't last long, but her friendship with Larry was friendly and caring. Each had similar interests. That was it. They'd go for walks together and maybe swim in the lake. Not much else. Then Larry got a girlfriend and told Bertha that he couldn't see her anymore. It was a sad, sad, sad situation. Bertha met quite a few Larrys over her years, each leaving a small heartbreak.

Bertha had no female friends. Neither did Heidi, Fiona, or Sabrina, at all. Oh, the ferocious issues around this matter. It was as though other women found her to be too strange to befriend. She was betrayed, beaten down, clawed, through scorn, envy, and credible dislike, for Dot had an air of "I'm better than you." Vicious, evil competition. First of all, they were jealous of her grades, then her looks, which complimented everything.

Fiona had only to smile, and every man would look her direction. That's all she would allow. Bertha was too wise to allow Heidi, who was a little bit retarded, to get hurt again. So she put up a blockade that no man could break down. They could talk, play music, laugh, and drink beer, but nobody could get to the golden Garden of Eden, the well-protected Dorothy, Dot.

Glittering and golden, with locks long and beautiful, she remained an enigma to all the Curtises and Dereks, who she had long since figured out and broken as easily as a toothpick. Her friendly Larrys were good reading partners, but they preferred to keep to themselves rather than be hurt by her again and again. If only there were a mature Cliff. Someone who could stand by her in anything and throughout everything. Maybe Santa Claus would bring her a grown-up Cliff. It was a sweet thought to dwell upon. Mainly, she kept her eyes open for the intelligent type with heart, soul, and mind of genuine character. She didn't want to waste any more time on fondling and feeling around here and there in this bed and that bed. Life had become so much more important, especially after having read the Bible.

At this point in life it was time for Bertha to have some restitution. It was her moment of reprise, her beginning of laughter, the swimming of thoughts in her head, the letdown of the blockade surrounding precious Dot. This was okay because Heidi, stiff as steel, surrounded her, protecting her from the outside willies. Her strength was incredible, having been through so much torture and so much damage to protect Dot. Now she had her, and no one was coming near who didn't have a pass from God, a faith in our Lord Jesus Christ. He is the only one who can protect her now and always will.

A little older now, Sabrina starts banging her head as her schizophrenia sets in. Sabrina, the lost and wandering imagination of Dot, has come alive like a radio switched on. The new pain begins here, even as Heidi tries to struggle against the odds of Willies, and Carrie catapults us everywhere in genius ways to figure out the one way that will lead out of the traps and the pursuit to damage and own this disfigured Dot. Such a squashed Fiona as she is crushed between Sabrina and the atmosphere, extending to Bertha, who cries out, the negligence, and Carrie tries to hide under Heidi, who must be strong now.

Heidi thrashes like a cat in water. The whales are after her to swallow her like Jonah in the Bible. She wants one way but gets another way. She smarts with pain as her head bangs against the wall. Ropes tie her up, and the men line up to have their way with her. When someone comes to the rescue, he roars and growls as he rips the chains from her swollen feet and tears the ropes from about her torso. Gently he carries her away and leads her to a place where there are nurses and doctors, healing psychologists, and psychiatrists.

Heidi wakes up from this new place, spewed by Jonah's whale, and looks around her. The sun comes in through a small window, and her bed is dry and clean.

Carefully cleaned off, she returns to her bed and lies there.

ABUSE

Tunnel vision greets Bertha as she opens her eyes, confused and distorted. No one is here that she knows. Who was her rescuer? It's a painful repose. Snatched away from there, God had sent a messenger to keep her from getting lost twice. This time losing her body, her one possession to the ruthless men that might have it for a little touch here and a little touch there. A leap from bed to bed. Little Sabrina shuddered at the fearsome situation she had narrowly escaped. What makes a rapist tick? Again and again and again. Even incest takes place in horrible situations, forced, and this no laughing matter. It is ruthless. It is despicable. The perpetrator seeks satisfaction in a sexual manner. Without regard for the sacred makeup of our God-given sexuality.

It's enclosed and repetitive. If it happens once, it will happen again unless there is intervention like Heidi, Dot's hero, who broke apart the assault on Dot's character, saving her from a life of deathly depression and self-hatred. No one who has been assaulted this way gets along well in life afterward. The negative aftershocks carry through life, but there is medical attention that can help the hurt individual. That's where physical doctors determine bodily damage and treat it. Then, there is much advanced psychology and psychiatry to help the individual psyche or mind/heart/spirit combination.

Unfortunately, rape goes unreported in many cases. Rape in mentally ill cases is reported even more rarely. Many turn a deaf ear. Or turn up an ignorant nose. Many people are too ashamed to talk about it, because pain still doesn't go away, and the everlasting wounded, ugly scars on character can be isolating.

Each has a specific story; let's get back to Dot's. She was surrounded by love by the time she found herself in a clinical institution. A strange case of schizophrenia, depression, generalized anxiety, colored with panic attacks, extreme loneliness, isolation, self-hatred, anger, hopelessness, frustration, patience, blight, crackup, flatness, empty head, overload, weight gain, general malaise, medical drowsiness, character, maturity, lack of understanding, truthful hatred, giving up too soon, violence, and many more attributes toward the illness that struck Dot at such a young age in University.

How to help Dot. Who is Dot? Dot hid herself behind the haze of Sabrina, who tried to make the staff feel good. Fiona got malicious and demanding about the lack of food and coffee, now in a psychiatric hospital, needing to obey clinical rules. Heidi opened herself wide and showed off her stunted beauty, while Fiona covered her with a blanket of truth. But there was anger there, steaming below the surface. Soon she was yelling at staff. They tied her down after she kicked a nurse, in self-defense, she said, and woke up in prison with Satan guarding her door. Then, while no one was looking, Satan slipped in, broke her arm temporarily as he raped her, then left, leaving Fiona on the bed, smiling giddily, picking bullets out of her peppered body.

Someone brought dinner in that cold, isolated room that evening, and she picked at it, but in her head, she consumed Satan, every last ounce of him. They were friends after that, and no one saw him in the hospital psychiatric ward again.

Get rid of him, get rid of him, her thoughts told her, but soon she started praying for prisoners everywhere, for people to have second or third chances, and the world was a place for everyone to everything. Terrible thoughts have consequences on our actions. Yet I, as Dot, can still have good feelings about myself, for self-love is the most beautiful and initial love of all, other than God's true love.

The love of Satan can only be explained by God's rule to love all, especially your enemies. In this case, you corrupt them. Breaking the barrier of hatred familiarizes us with the intensity of our youth and the need to build strong backbones for later on in life.

We must learn to love what we do not love, or we will never discover a way to overcome it. And this is not insidious or sneaky, for love is true and cannot be broken. Wipe the towel on the dishes, and hang up the towel after the shower. But don't forget to thank God for the good things in life, like the Good Book that instructs on the ways to get through this life unscathed. This is what saved Bertha out of Jonah's whale. She landed directionless, dropkicked into nowhere in life, the details of which are not necessary because they are variable, and landed among perverts who would eat of her innocence if they could. If it wasn't for her Savior, if it wasn't for her Christ.

Heidi was exceptionally happy for Christ, and she was the most expressive about this too. She rained down regularly on people, questioning their faith if they were Catholic and if they were Quaker Catholic. Fiona had never thought of herself as Catholic, but in this healing institution her mind twisted and she thought strange things. One could say she was bedeviled.

Fiona was quiet and she was loud. Her feet were cold, she wanted socks, and no one would bring her any. Finally, after enough nagging, the nurse brought her nice, big, white tube socks that Bertha and Heidi treasured as they hugged each other. They were the biggest, softest, warmest socks she'd ever seen, and she sat cross-legged on her bed just staring at them.

Dot's temper flared as she scowled at those ugly men still staring at her. What did they want, and why would they not leave her alone? Why? Her tears came at last when finally she broke and all kinds of beliefs arose in her mind. In her mind, Dot had lost her mother, who took a bullet in the face in order to save Dot's life. She hugged herself and wept quietly, massaging her legs and caressing her toes.

"Well, at least Mom is set free," she surmised, and a hawk outside her window became Mom reincarnated to visit whenever needed and to prove that she was happy as a hawk.

But not long after, Mom visited in the hospital. That's where she was realized by Carrie, who was busy taking care of logistics in every circumstance.

The ground carrier was foolish enough to trip over every now and again, for there were flaws in the shoes that fit those precious feet on Dot's body. In her mind, those precious feet had been cut off twice. Twice. She remembered sitting futilely in the corner of her kitchen at home, hugging herself, as the stumps of her legs where her feet had been bled painfully all around her. She took garlic and smashed it with a hammer in the middle of the floor. That would chase the alien evil away. She awoke, the kitchen was gone, and a nurse stood by her bed, offering water with a cup of pills.

Those pills were an evil in themselves, until feisty, shameful Dot realized they were good for her; they helped. Hideous Dot had to make the final decisions now. No one could stop her. Not after the prison cell and her adieu with Satan. He was her friend, a courier.

Peaceful and brave, also extremely shy. Shameful asunder, there were only two loopholes. First of all, there was shame as to the sex and murder in her life. Then came the revelation of her private parts, the revelation of her private journals, those treasure chests of well-thought-out wisdom and creativity. Painful reprise, negligence, and record of a rare walk of life.

Those poor old journals she should have torn up or burned in the fire. Hot, hot fires. Oh well...so they were found out. Someone found her out. Scrabbling Dot, scribbling page after page through all her pain, her early years of schizophrenia, where she would talk little to anyone, her family to the utmost, and her stomping psychiatrist, who could not let her ride around on fairy tales but glued her to the truth of her condition that she was born to bear, and nobody knew why.

He was a smart psychiatrist and knew well how to handle an angry, crying lady in her twenties suffering the realities of her disease. The denial, the hatred, the desperation, and the need for retaliation. He was able to parry all her darts and gently lead her on an educational route that would train her in many ways to take care of herself, pruning herself in all areas of life to be able to fit into some notch somewhere.

It was important, but not embarrassing with Dr. Stomp Feet, as she renamed him after the hospital experience. Yes, Big Foot made a fine doctor. In many ways that were strictly medical, all parts of Dot were familiar with her doctor. By this time she'd been in his care for over fifteen years, and he knew her quite well. Doctor Stomp Feet is a pillar in Dot's life, though just a small box of a window in each month. God must have pulled a good one out of his pocket.

He came to know her family and worked closely with them. Step-by-step baby Bertha needed to know how to grow into precious Carrie, who could cling to Heidi, still striving for Fiona and dreaming of Sabrina. These were all her Band-Aids. These were her weapons, her defense system against the outside world, who would navigate her through any limited type of day. It was learning the limits of life that were most painful. Bumping into them again and again and again, each time shattering any bit of gained ego.

Her confidence was zilch, and this is what caused Heidi to finally create Fiona. Her surrounding of suave nonchalance and somewhat aloof behavior quickly calculated through every circumstance to navigate through every day, night, and moment.

Her Creator caused her to do it. He couldn't let her do it, just die in a suit of armor that did not fit? Barely fitting into this uncomfortable armor anyhow, Heidi was encouraged to grow in confidence, and this hurt because of how painful the growing process is.

Heidi liked to play with Fiona, at home when family members visited with friends and she shined her "I am beautiful" light. Just for a while, because getting in too deep deserved putting out, and this she could not do, so thank God and Jesus and the Holy Spirit that she had a bedroom at the end of the hall.

Living with Fiona hurt Dot, so Sabrina appeared out of necessity; a way to monitor affections without getting hurt every time. Moving through life, things happen, and something huge happened to Dot. She became pregnant.

She found new strength, and new loss, as the baby had to be put up for adoption. Schizophrenic Dot could not raise a child on her own. She knew sadness then. Sabrina held everything together and did the only thing she knew she could do, giving the little bundle of perfection up for adoption. The devastated Dot fell into Sabrina's arms, who cuddled her like her own child.

Sabrina played Mama to Dot, who cried and cried and was stopped each time by Sabrina from hurting herself at all. She grew to accept. Her personal diary became mental, for ruination of her life must not happen again like it did before.

The devil played with her life like a harmonica. So she learned to dance with his tunes. The night in the prison when he had accepted Dot was enough to keep the significance of her ego back into the picture. He cared; he even loved her. If he cried a tear, she never saw it. Perhaps his pain was too great from having lived all his life in hell…the planet Mercury.

He danced too, a funny dance where he lifted each foot quickly as though it was avoiding a burn. Flames must be hot in hell.

Sabrina glowed in rapture as she floated gently around this strange figure from hell. Neither smiled nor made any facial expression. Yet each could feel the other's heart. Feelings and emotions were dealt with tenderly. But they were soon to part, each knowing, and each retracted into respective selves, each to its own self.

Time went by, and the closeness was soon forgotten,

but not the honor and affiliation. Both respected each other and now and then made contact.

Helplessly alone in the world, to the point of self-destruction, there was little for Fiona to go on in those early years after quitting college. First, there were the powerful feelings of failure. Then came the powerful camouflage of silent envy. Too much was never too much for her. She would just fall back and break apart, silent tears and noisy howls emanating from different parts of the house on different days. Hot tears. Her glasses needed washing twice daily to cleanse them of the spattered teardrops.

To make matters worse, the medicines made exercise that much more difficult, despite making mental functions flower just a little each day. Fiona's body grew weak, and simple runs left her wheezing and gasping like never before. But Fiona did not give up; she knew that she always felt better after a little walk, and so she made a daily practice of walking the dog. A new feature arose. Fear of other people she passed as she walked along. How to hide? Where to run? In the end she was forced to learn to say hi or to decide whether or not to make eye contact.

This was a confusing issue that Fiona talked to with Dr. Stomp Feet about. When to make eye contact and when not to. When to shake hands and when not to. Dr. Stomp Feet even suggested that Fiona was physically, mortally affected by people approaching from fifty feet away. This was during a time when Fiona was trying to go back to school because she should, not because she could.

Mountains of molehills gathered up around Sabrina, and she had to start digging. First of all, her life was going nowhere, apparently. Significantly, there was no focus to her schooling, and her only function was a Friday-night Christian fellowship group she had discovered, where she discovered more and more of her shortcomings, all the social failures that she had.

Fiona made flowers out of friends. They bloomed and then died. Maybe she couldn't water them right, or her skies were so gloomy they never let the sunshine through that every relationship requires. Maybe it was too one-sided. Maybe Fiona faked it too easily, and then judgment fell as she would let a lonesome insult fall. A "you're so much better than me, because…" Then she would twist around before gaining reward or a counteract. Sabrina was the queen of any such punishment who stood a head higher than anyone around her, with just enough time to back out of a situation without Heidi being found out for disrespectful behavior. Heidi was coercive and disrespectful but only when she felt the pain of being laughed at.

That was pain. And pain could escalate. When Derek came on to the scene, there was added embarrassment. No doubt she had good looks and attracted good attention. Heidi was a lure, Fiona was a queen who fanned others gently with her feathers, and Sabrina came up with difficult questions that no one could answer. This would shock the tease, and Dot could slip out unnoticed as the banter went on and she hung her torn head with grief, refusing to use the bathroom, not wanting to see the face, this face of a doll of mischief.

Dot knew better than to chase after other men. She'd had her go with more than one Curtis, Derek, and Larry. She couldn't get hurt by them any more, and they could no more make a fool of her life. Besides, by now she'd read the entire Bible and learned to set her sights on higher things, namely on God and his Son, Jesus, and the Holy Spirit.

These were the things that were important to her. Not Curtis anymore. He only teased her and dropped her again and again, because Heidi was defenseless against emotionally grown-up guys. Or so they may seem, but that's a whole different story.

They carried her away and left her. They failed to show up at her doorstep. They didn't answer her futile phone calls. Heidi cleaned the house vigorously, although not obsessively. She started and finished book after book after book. Finally, she started writing diaries on an old Apple computer. Writing came easily to her. Both handwritten journals and typewritten journals. She began to discover something. She had something to say after all.

After going for years under the name of "boring," or "nothing there," and trying hard to cover up this tragedy, she analyzed a missing factor of her personality: the verbal ability to express but not feel thoughts. Emotional verbiage. Whatever the disability, she *did* have something there; the only way to express it was through writing and touch. The words poured out of her, and with the help of Big Foot she began to understand this anomaly and put a name to it. It was simply schizophrenia. I can talk. But I read much better. I, Dot, have learned to converse better by being in all kinds of difficult situations. Dr. Stomp Feet has urged me to talk about my feelings, a healing magic that can only be applied if well intentioned on both sides. Doctors really do heal. They have the know-how; they are "ordained" and blessed.

Blessed are those who come into a good relationship that withstands the ups and down.

FUTILITY

Organization tendency is a rapturous quiz, freak sort of nature that means a lot more than just reaching out. It is giving up on the fight to realize that you are different and not everybody is fair to everybody. We all have our differences, and so does Fiona. She is the main outlet of expression for words that represent emotions. It's very klutzy and hard to maintain. Bertha comes to the rescue sometimes, but she can't show her mottled face for long. She needs privacy to keep her thoughts together.

Sometimes thoughts are scattered everywhere, and there can be a time to gather them as well. Some thoughts we wish we never had and are truly invasive. They haunt and follow and tease and destroy. They break down our self-image and give us false ideas about ourselves.

Sometimes we hate ourselves, we can't help it, and nature knows that there is no hope for the future of generative thoughts, for they are capped off after teasing and tormenting the victim. There is nothing so great as an evil thought that is overcome. We hold ourselves gently and enter gently from one situation to another. We overcome betrayal; we outwit self-bashing.

Amazingly enough, we can try different approaches to conquering unwanted thoughts, thoughts that want us to do ourselves harm. It is the pain of conquering that is so significant. Our attitudes are the best meters that judge our thoughts. Are we great? Are we evil? Is our pain our own faults or a hidden perpetrator in the shadows who has but a nasty voice in Fiona's head?

Rash and defiant, they are like insects crawling all over her body. This is a moodiness that can be understood by the schizophrenic. Fiona wheezes and coughs and chokes on nothing but a nasty will-force that is attempting to take over her calling of help. Help that will cover the nasty blights on her personality where Bertha let go because she could no longer hold on to her string of privacy through Dot while being bombarded by invasive thoughts, also known as thought insertion.

This is the most painful part of schizophrenia, being unable to control your own thoughts as they sneak up on you. But believe it or not, there are good ways to deal with them. You can ignore them, blame them, talk back to them, and even trick them out of you. The best thing to do is to not believe, as you learn to discern between your own thoughts and inserted thoughts that come from somewhere else.

The schizophrenic personality grows and changes as time passes. Joining the army makes you strong; battling schizophrenia makes you strong. Strong and suicidal, yet with the will to go on. There are many places to be, but right here right now is the most popular place to be. Otherwise you get carried away by imaginary thoughts, and people don't know how to hang onto sanity in the way of law. Dwelling is the fierce substitute for standing on solid ground, but you can still get lost in history.

Very many people get confused, and they don't know why. The problem is decision making. Making clear decisions for solid reasons is logical on the basis that abuse and misuse of medicines can be fatal, although some cause a temporary high.

Pleasant thoughts are real, and they come through because Fiona has witnessed pleasant events and peaceful serenity. The good of the world is real, and Heidi, clinging to Fiona, can keep peaceful, thoughtful outlooks on the real vision of life, the vision that comes from the heart.

Pure visions of the heart cannot be perverted. It is the mind that grows distorted and puts things out of position, keeping deathly, most awesome, and disgusting thoughts at bay but allowing them to play havoc with the material of the mind. The mind is the most intricate place where faulty beginnings are located. Sinister thoughts originate here. They grow here and fester like disease until they reach down and attack emotions where Heidi boxes herself around Dot to protect her, and Bertha exudes innocence to remind Heidi of the innocence that would bolster Heidi's feeble morale.

It exists, because baby Dot, before the birth of Bertha, was totally innocent, found in her garbage can crying. She's innocent, just imbalanced, wanted by both good and evil all through her life. The hardest blow hit when Heidi drowned in social amnesia, or arrested development, and she was no longer able to communicate normally. No friends, and that was the hardest part at Stanford University. Being around a lot of people does not make it so you're not lonely. Loneliness is the basis of most psychiatric illnesses. People reach out for help, and arms just aren't long enough to find help. Nobody notices the withdrawal. It is a pain beyond despair. Nobody reaches back or lingers; it is a societal deficiency, and the need for help is commonly overlooked.

The cry for help is silenced by hidden emotions unable to be expressed. Recorded violent action is the most recognizable cry for help, even when it ends up with people getting hurt. The grace of crime is the deepest root of its existence, a scream of pain that has not been helped.

The recurrence of this situation brings added toughness to the new bout of promotion within internal configuration of exuberance and clownish activity that cannot be understood, a gibberish known as "word salad." Heidi is the clown most misunderstand, for she is so good at imitation in most circumstances but not in internal circumstances, where activity has taken place that keeps out forgotten images of times that once were sunny days on a private beach.

Who knows what goes on in private circumstances? Where did Fiona learn her morals and ethics? Did she disappear one night and wake up an android? Why did nobody see where she went?

She shriveled into a nobody and would have disappeared if it had not been for the creation of Sabrina, who fell in like a guardian angel and intimidated the predators for the work they tried to put down upon her. Sabrina knew about work, and she came prepared to do good work. Work that would change and preserve the life of Dot. Miserable as she was, Dot lay innocent and weeping at the bottom of a well, a well of her own tears, which eventually buoyantly buoyed her up to the top, where her tears became tears of hope and ran over the top, fertilizing the lawn of the dream home where she would one day live. One day...

Dreams. Dreams are a means of hanging on to hope. And even at this point there are dreams in everyone's head. Wishes, hopes, desires of innocence, love, respect, and challenge. Peace is another blessing that blows in alongside of hope. There are still times when Dot cries about the pain she's been through, and sometimes it still hurts too much.

The wayside is where we all fall when the ditch is too near and calculations are not correct as we navigate our course through life. The ditch is so dear and near to us. It's a place to grovel in self-pity and let dreams go, pretending we have not heard of them. But ground to sky, there is always space to go on thinking in the manner of start to stop. Bringing it all to a finish, we get washed away when the rains fill ditches to their brims and we get washed out like worms on the wayside.

Sneaking through life is no good either. Wherever you are, you will someday be discovered, whatever the state of your condition. Plus, this is a reason to work on continually bettering yourself. Don't you want to be on your best as you are discovered? Impossible. Everybody gets beaten down and atrocious.

It's hard to be looking good all the time. No matter when or if you are discovered. True life comes, is, and not all are prepared for a fine introduction. Because different things are special in everybody. Some people wear globs of makeup, spend great deals of time on their hair, and spend on costly wardrobes that are recycled through the seasons. Others are more simple and don't care quite so much about facial appearance and first impressions. It could be a matter of confidence or insecurity, negligence in childhood, or a cruel, teasing amount of deficiency of self-control. Sometimes you can never get or do enough.

Aggravating as it is, there is too much emotional involvement in the way we look today. It is better to be simple than gaudy and better to be nice than naughty.

Brace yourself for the truth, for the reasons that people fall in ditches and let go of the road. The future is too grave. Hopelessness is wound up in knowledge of death and failure. Why try when pain is so adamant and effort so futile? Or so it seems. Effort never leads to failure. It leads to experience and knowledge. It helps to thicken a weak and frail skin. Naughtiness is infernal and a device of the underworld. The Antichrist. It is what happens when teasing and misleading cause misconduct in new and old chambers of commerce that surround efforts of misconduct in a train of bitter infatuation. It leads the way, and money rises as the most important thing in the world.

Bitter tabulations lead to pounding on the head and reminders that we are weak and we are small. It is the universe that was created large and unimaginable. Why? So that we can keep wondering and ever growing in the right directions as we fail and learn from our mistakes and from our successes. And what are we growing for? Each person has a right to arise from the depths, to keep from falling into ditches, and to design a future that is not so grave. The future is victorious, and we don't know why, only that the human race is a triumphant race in this world of chasing victories and handling corruptions.

Worrying about each other is a way of joining hands in victory. Hands come in many colors, and joining all is a celebration of life. What we want to watch out for and remove are the hands that hold small knives that slice and kill instead of clasping in goodness.

It all sounds so good and bad, but that's what it is. That Antichrist has an armor we can easily defuse, and that is our willpower, which he tries to control. He begs for mercy when he is found out, when the smallest crime is stopped.

That is where experience plays good, and the ditches can be praised for the failures we have overcome in pain and envy, perversion, and misleading. Where growth leads to the level of the pain of atrocious birthing in

Fiona, there is absolutely no more leveling out the small mountains. Instead our energy is spent in climbing over them or going around. Enough of trying to change our world. Better to be a stump in a lake than to try to drain the lake and let the stump dry out for no purpose. The world will change, but on its own as we change. Fiona marks the challenge of growth in ourselves and the experience of happiness in the way of schizophrenia that has aspects similar to the lives of many ordinary people in a much smaller degree and greater population.

Fiona is made strong in carrying the load given by schizophrenia. Her mental muscle is a great asset, made powerful and awesome, like the body of a great athlete. Only what gives Fiona her pizzazz, or her wild character, is her ability to deal with the underworld, the ability to deal with dilemmas that ordinarily people wouldn't dream of trying to do. Do? Would you try to stay underwater as long as a whale? Would you try to walk down the street where everybody is looking at you, talking about you, and devising ways to overthrow you before you can cross the street at the other side? Would you refuse to jump off a building if a seductive voice kept telling you, with honey, that the Promised Land lay right ahead of you? What if you could see it? Schizophrenia can be deadly with the right words in depressed people.

What if the voices invading your head, as they did to Fiona, tried to persuade you to stab your little sister to death? Fiona had a love policy. She grew up in a family of love and always refrained from hurting people, and so she was able to talk to her belligerent self about it, refraining from the attack and going to bed instead, where an alarmed Heidi lay weeping over her torturous condition.

Belligerent self is something I have not yet touched on. In the "me, myself, and I" trio, the me and the I are innocent. Myself, or the self, is always the troublemaker and disagrees with everything. That is what makes decision making so difficult. "I can't agree with myself on this. Maybe I should, but what if I can't? I'm not good enough (for myself). I did it myself." We see that the self is the central figure of a greedy conglomerate person. Fiona's self is Heidi. Heidi's ego is Fiona. Fiona's superego, or conscience, is Sabrina, and her whole person, including Bertha and Carrie, is a psychotic, schizophrenic dilemma. Proud of herself for all the work she's done on herself. Heidi is strong as an oak stump. No one can knock her down; she is already attached to heaven, with a latch that will not rust, break, disintegrate, or fall apart. This is the hope that Bertha clings to as she nervously watches herself sway back and forth in the wind.

Sabrina is so tall and nonchalant. Will anyone call her bluff? Not if she is fast enough and disappears into an invisible Heidi, who can fend off anything by the guts that so many times have been contorted within her.

The pain is all there with her irritable bowel syndrome, arising out of mixed up and twisted emotions, shaken up and torn with futility into a mass of constant healing where damage from chewing emotions has been done. Self-consumption is a way of suicide. A way to destroy the self before it has had a chance to express its pain.

Suicidal tendencies are common in the way of

schizophrenia. A misunderstood disease, there is commonly an overlooked aspect of *pain* that will not go away on its own. All kinds of pain. Physical pain and emotional pain. Mental pain and inner turmoil. No one can wait till it goes away. But it has to be dealt with, because it *is* there.

Left alone it festers, and people act out and do violent things. These are the mistreated freaks you hear about on TV who have not had proper treatment and are unable to have proper conduct in situations that push pain buttons that bring on pain and madness. Memory and reality equate to make moment to moment, where brushfires look like warm beds, and the alcohol bottle gets smashed to the pavement when it is emptied at last.

There are those who seek help at a young age, the age when the disease most often strikes like a rattlesnake, unexpected and undeserved. It is unfair. No one should have to suffer as Fiona does, who has become a rather good expert at taking care of herself. Sometimes the voices come and try to lead her away on the wrong track, and she has become quite adept at recognizing voices in her head, especially those that mean to take her to harm, where Sabrina the sorceress would become food for the Antichrist.

Cursed be the Antichrist who would fool anyone it could into believing that it meant well. It is usually addictive. It wants food. Lost souls. Unbelievers. Those who don't take it seriously.

Christ knows better. We can all do better than eat the meat fit for the king. He is holy, and his Word is great enough for us to chew on. The Word is the way; it leads to our needs and cares for our tendencies of wit. The Word is the greatest aspect of life, the filter between nonentity and existence. We are servants here, those of us who can acknowledge it. That's when eye contact means something, and Fiona no longer has to look away.

Bubbling anger is a good indicator that evil had been discovered, and a plan for evil is being meant for you. Fiona knows this. People don't always know when they're just being used for no good purpose. Furthering of the Kingdom is what means something to most, even though they don't recognize it. Work means something; it satisfies the need to be active working. Work is the meaning of life. Food for work, and work for food.

Help people who can't work. They can be encouraging. All deserve a good life, even the disabled people who have severe schizophrenia and have not learned to work well with it. Their work is getting through each day, doing the basics of life, the eating, activity, hygiene, medicine schedule, and sleep.

Those who know can help those who don't, or who won't admit that the problem lies with them. It is an internal disease that sometimes does or doesn't have affect, a word used to describe unusual behavior that stands out as different or weird to the common eye.

The common eye is a disease in itself—part of schizophrenia. The eye can tell so much. A person's mood, a lie, a happy spell, depression, anger…the list goes on. Eyes can see into each other. Sometimes they meet, sometimes they avert. Fear of knowledge, fear of the truth.

Fear of the ugliness that the schizophrenic feels within. All eyes are on Fiona wherever she goes, but Sabrina has learned to defend this position by an amazing tactic. Instead of avoiding every eye, she picks and chooses and meets gazes with people here and there.

Taking part in life just a little bit leads to further participation in communal life. The schizophrenic has every right to live on this earth, perhaps more right than other bad sorts of people who have no right to be violent out of malice and hatred. That is unfair to even the unheard who need help to feel needed. Creation and wisdom come from excursions in the underworld that are finished triumphantly and are valuable to everybody. The bottom line is that everybody has some sort of psychosocial problem they're dealing with on some level, and weakness comes to us in the parts that are painful. These parts we hide and disguise. These are the parts we live with and must learn to overcome in order to blossom and live a fruitful life.

These are failings and futility. Our weaknesses and tendencies follow seductive paths toward sinning, acting in ways that are not wholesome for the person, the place, and the attitude involved.

Giving up is the worst situation, but there is always hope. The fighter is the winner, and the loser has no hope. The chances are that hope slips away from the winner when attitudes grow into grotesque masks of unparalleled envy. This is when showing off grows into a condition of the mind, and we forget where it comes from.

From the front, from the back, from the sides, top,

or bottom, all illusions come when we believe our own ego is bigger than the bites that the world can send in any given situation. It is a plot, a need to grow bigger and better than your neighbor, rather than simplicity in remaining your neighbor's friend.

Everyone is given one life to live, and what you do with that life is how you paint it in the end when God hands you the paints and the brushes and says, "Show me." Here we falter, and God takes the paints away before we can begin. But whatever the case, life passes before your eyes in the most unusual situation. Death. It comes to everybody and has no hold on anyone. It is just another doorway, one that we complain and worry about, yet without it we would not try to do our best.

When we do our best, God smiles, knowing that his creation is imperfect and how beautiful is the outcome of the conglomeration of people in his world. The beauty of expression, if only there were others to believe. The time is short, the hope is long, and we can only do so much in a given lifetime. Helping people makes the picture even more beautiful. Acceptance, unusual change of attitude, arguments that turn out to be blessings.

Very careful are those who see their life wasting away, and with the prompting of the Holy Spirit they seek help. Oh dear God, don't let me be a failure at death. I don't want to have been a failure at life.

Seeking blessings is like fishing out of a fish hatchery. It just isn't fair for those waiting out at sea who seek the salmon runs each year. Those who are blessed have been rewarded for deeds done well and attitudes that are helpful to other people, clinging to the multitudes where the powerful goodness of blessings can rain down in the full force of each of God's added luxuries.

Forceful issues come crashing down when people get hurt. How to resolve these issues without forcing the dilemma on other people as well. Funneling feelings from here to there keep the bad away from the good so that a storm doesn't blow up when they meet. That's why most issues are dealt with little by little. In unusual circumstances, all feelings come to bear at the same time, and we are in for the lightning storm of life.

Fiona decided to test life by going off her schizophrenic medications. She believed, she *knew* that it would work, and that everyone around her was crazy, not her. The end result turned out to be a five-month stay in a psychiatric ward. She had so many problems that all reacted at once. She was taken away and brought to the hospital, where a certain kind of healing began. Fiona's favorite thing to do was play the piano. Every random set of notes was a melodic prayer. She was very religious and extremely violent at having been put in a corner at last. Fight or flight. The time finally came to fight. Heidi is no longer a "wimp"; she was taken down not without kicking and screaming, a hellish noise and every kick, punch, struggle, jerk, and pull fought through her body as they yanked her down and pushed her to the floor. That was all. The rest I have already mentioned. This is the prehistory of finding herself in prison, with Satan watching at her door. What follows has formed a new kind of friendship based on trust.

PUSH AND PULL

Some people get mad at little things and react to them, making them slightly annoying to be around. Others save up their anger to the point of uncontrollable outbursts that frighten everybody and can make them dangerous to be around. Love is what we need, even if it has to be from a confined distance. So it is in the hospital. These people are skilled at dealing with outbursts of behavior, and, on the other hand, they encourage good behavior by things such as art therapy groups, pet therapy, and one-on-one counseling. All in all, the toughest part is getting patients to take their medicines three times a day because out of the hospital that will be the patient's own responsibility.

Time and quiet quality of the passing days is what remains so healing. There is a daily regimen of quality activity and encouragement toward good behavior urged by forced behavior. Being forced down onto my bed to get shots in my lower back was the punishment of refusing to take my medication.

Then there were all the religious imaginings, the codependent issues that I faked with spirits only I knew were there. I shot bullets out of my gun, fashioned as my fingers formed it. I even ran around taking bullets for other people in this gallant war, because I had the special power of being able to squeeze bullets out of my body, and I didn't want to lose the ones I loved. I learned who to love and who to hate.

Then there were the chameleon killers that nothing could kill unless you peed on them and covered the pee with a blanket. The next step would be to toss those blankets out of the room and slam my door as hard as I could. This always made a refreshing loud *bam* as the next door down would slam from the force of my door closing so hard.

Behind that door, nobody knew what was going on, especially as I napped and snoozed and gazed out of the window, watching the gigantic waterfall pouring into the river down below and the wasp nest snuggled into the corner of the pane.

I cried hard, I laughed and laughed, and killed people right and left as they disturbed me in my reverie. Something about peeing on the floor was extremely satisfying. Racing with Jesus down the hall was the most fun thing I ever did. This taught me faith and the meaning of reality. It is where you are when you are. Reality is now, later, and before. It never goes away, because we are caught up in an eggshell that catches you like spider webs if you try to escape. Even suicide has a jettison hatch. No one wants someone who will not continue in reality. This hurts God. It rejects him, as we reject ourselves. If others kill us, that is not suicide; it is making conditions of life unbearable that no one could survive willingly in such a circumstance.

Try and try and try again. Each time the outcome is different, better or worse, a learning process. A way to grow and manifest our human powers as we excel in areas made especially for us. You can learn as you grow, and as you grow you can contribute, even if life is difficult in all aspects and it takes that last bright star to make you hold on, just to wonder why it is there and how it got there, to believe that there is a power greater out there, and there are good things we can pursue. Of course we trip and stumble into roadblocks; we lose confidence and break our hearts. God makes us inferior in our minds, only to remind us that we can grow and become the leader inside of ourselves, not to eternally remain the underdog in the area of our life where you feel most weak.

Weakness is not bad. It is just a place to work on, to strengthen, and to treat tenderly. Where would tenderness be if we could not learn to love ourselves? That is the beginning factor. The place in life where we stop depending on others for everything, and learn to put ourselves out there, where we can be seen and acknowledged as an individual, beautiful and contrite.

Your hair can be long or short, your skin dark or light,

your eyes brown, blue, or green. And that does make you different. We are not all the same, no matter what they say. Each person does a different thing in life, even if that means being completely dependent due to infirmity. You cause people to care, because you count. You count; you really do, no matter who you are.

Carrie began to realize that after Bertha began to complain about her heavy load. She was born green, grew up brown, and then fell into childhood blonde and tan. Little Carrie went everywhere her brothers and sisters went. She was bonded to them in a way that kept her from learning to socialize with others.

Carrie's family was very close-knit, and due to the tragic circumstance of her childhood, she clung to her parents and her sisters and brothers. The bond didn't appear strange or different. Nobody noticed her quiet, demure behavior. She was pretty beyond compare. She played with her sisters.

She chased and played with her brothers. There was nothing wrong with that. Skip Carrie and we get to Heidi. Heidi had to go to school. Heidi had to pretend to socialize. She had no real friends. Her world was dark and hoary, lined with crappie music and hours of imagining the way it could be if only it would be, but it wasn't.

Carrie lost her best friend, the only best friend she ever had, who turned her back on her and left when her family moved away. This was total and complete trauma for Carrie. She'd loved her friend who now was gone, but who'd betrayed her a few years earlier. Carrie tried to pretend that the friendship was still there, but it wasn't.

Even Heidi was disgusted with this circumstance and tried to pull Carrie out, but Carrie never grew up; she faded into darkness as Heidi grew out of her, skin so thick that even crying on her bed or in the high school bathrooms was normal. Nobody knew her, except for Cliff, who she did happen to bump into after all these years again. Cliff and Heidi were boyfriend and girlfriend, so close. Heidi could confide in him, and he did all the high school things with her, like going to dances, parties, dates, exploring sex, and having wild fun at the beach house that Heidi's parents owned. She had fun with her sisters, their shared friends, and together they laughed, talked, drank beer, swam, and played in the sun or by the fire at night. Windsurfing was especially fun, and so was fishing or a friendly game of badminton. Books were friendly too, and the sisters shared with friends at parties with beer, water, and beach fires.

Cliff and Heidi were an admirable couple, except that Heidi could not really socialize with anyone else. She could trust no one else; she'd been betrayed so many times because of her good looks and severely shy demeanor. Ever since Bertha was hurt as a little girl, Heidi trusted no one, even before she was born; she was being designed.

Heidi trusted her sisters, but she knew where the boundaries were and where she should and shouldn't go with them. She always needed an escape hatch.

That's when the raping began. Heidi got stuck at a party one night when Cliff had to leave, and Heidi thought she could still have fun. Her sisters were having fun. Cliff went home, and Heidi suddenly realized that there was no fun for her. She woke up the next morning in the back of a white van with two guys who were trying to put her clothes on. The memory was so painful. She was told not to tell anybody anything, seriously. She didn't. Heidi was dropped off at home, and she didn't call Cliff.

Heidi became dark and hurt. She could never tell Cliff what was wrong, because she never knew what was wrong. She was just more quiet than usual, and that meant nearly silent. Still Cliff was able to draw her out. He loved her dearly. He knew the real Heidi. By the time that Fiona came through, Heidi had already most foolishly broken Cliff's heart by getting together with someone at Stanford and telling Cliff about it at the end of her first college year. Cliff was never seen again, except at a couple of painful meetings when Heidi tried to struggle into Fiona, but Fiona had already bashed Heidi's relational face in.

It hurt like hell, especially when this infatuation utterly consumed her. She was thrown into a blender with him and was blended into a pathetic mess. This jerk, we might say, tended to the cocktail and slowly drank her down in an alcohol refreshment that parted her legs and gave up every study to spend every possible minute with him, in pure need-infatuated attachment.

This was only the beginning of a life of sexual suicide. Sex didn't matter; it just happened, and poor little Bertha committed suicide over and over again, but she could not complete the act, because Heidi forbade it.

Saucy and suave, deep alluring eyes, she could attract from across the room, but then she never knew what to do,

and that is how Fiona came forth, by carefully watching
an imitating the girls around her. She could not laugh as
they did. She watched and stared and escaped when it
was her turn. Exercise was her greatest escape, and her
aggression poured out of her sweat and muscle fatigue.

Everyone thought she was such a beautiful, athletic
warrior, and no one understood her academic media.
It was generally known that Fiona seemed to use time
watching and playing and doing crew, where she could
release her painful energy. Those college days did not
find many hours of studying for Fiona. Did she spend
too much time with the guys, or by herself? She blacked
out one too many times. Then one day it happened. Her
roommate called her a whore, leading on all the guys
and then dumping them before anything got serious.
That was the only place that felt like home, and it was
absolutely mandatory to break off the relationships before
they got too deep. Fiona was deep, and Heidi demanded
that deep, dark secrets remain that way, until finally even
Sabrina forgot what they were, feeling dark and scarred
in her flurry of life, coming and going from love to fear
to retreat.

Fiona was unable to do her homework. She started
taking schizophrenia pills and soon after gained thirty
pounds, which is a massive body self-image change at
such a young age. Young girls in college usually experience
a little weight gain, but thirty pounds plus, contorted
images, and swollen eyeballs were enough to laugh at
by anyone. How ugly, since Fiona had never learned to

communicate, and now she could no longer depend upon her looks to see her through.

That was that. With much moaning and shrieking on the phone to home, Fiona was allowed a medical leave of absence from Stanford University halfway through her second year of study. And what did she study? Other people's actions, reactions, and motivations.

Fiona's dad picked her up as they threw all her stuff into boxes and they exited the campus. *Bye-bye to the jerks and all you glaring, staring, stupid, cocky people. Don't you get it?*

Jenny Craig stepped into the picture, and Fiona lost her thirty-three pounds over a year and a half of painful dieting. Special techniques she learned in the required classes. Simple techniques that she remembers today. Techniques such as parking far from the store, using stairs, or sitting down twenty minutes when you get home before going directly to the refrigerator, and getting moderate daily exercise.

Her terrible eating disorder passed after a year or two, sending her to shopping mall food courts and dot-to-dot food suction spots. It was miserable. Food became Fiona's only friend as she came into the world. Her other great friend was sleep. Reading books gradually became a companion. All kinds of books from *Gone with the Wind* to *Jonathan Livingston Seagull,* to the entire *Holy Bible.* Sabrina knew that on days when she was able to read, these were the good days. Days grew better when Fiona started to go for walks. She loved to walk her dog, and she loved to jog with a Walkman attached to her ears at the park nearby.

Walking remained possible, but jogging became impossible due to cell damage from her medicines. Huge weight gain that came later on made life impossible for jogging. Her joints just couldn't handle the extra weight.

These are sad and serious issues, since Heidi always was a good athlete. It was this background that helped her to push through that part of her life, where gritting her teeth and hanging on, crying tears of blood, agonizing over every movement and thought, a slow, decrepit mausoleum of dead abilities, attitudes, and behaviors.

Dead, skeletal, obsolete behaviors left to decrepit facial expressions and painful frowns that forgot how to grin, which left smiling gone.

Bitter, disastrous, horrible, and cruel feelings that left strange behavior far behind. It was better then, to have no behavior at all, than to be judged by affective behavior. Best of all was to hide in the bedroom, in the radio, in the CD player, listening to favorite songs over and over and over again, and then wondering if I was wrong,

Skepticism and null behavior, tagging along, whining, complaining, but the emotional pain was real; it scarred as it passed by and left windows of hatred open to the awesome evil worlds she passed through.

Anxious and destitute, she ate the bitter remains of dinner after everyone else had eaten, because it was impossible to eat with other people. Strange, but the aftereffect made most everything acceptable.

Creeping around in the dark when everyone was gone

was terrifying all alone. No one there, no one to count on. Just a dog. A very good dog at that, even if he was naughty, had an eating disorder, growled at neighbors, and was stubborn on the leash. Sometimes one could tug three tons before he would budge an inch from an interesting scent.

Bumper Sticker is what I called him after he got hit by a car in the rear end. Luckily there was no serious damage. What that dog was to Fiona. What a friend, if ever there were a tugging, sniffing, pulling friend.

It was quiet in that big, old house, alone for days on end. My schizophrenia was wielding its way through the days and hours and minutes, as there was no real safety net within the safety net. That was the emptiness of this world.

That was the falling through into hell, where Fiona became an angel of the dark for a short time only, but a solid three years at that. Glaring, pulling, yanking, tug-a-tug-a-tug-a-boat. Let the little belly float. Baby born so soon, makes no sense just look at the moon. Too fat by the clock, too thin, and then wanting to gain weight again.

Like a butterfly dancing through the darkness, dodging all the obstacles, there is a kind of mirage where one comes back to the body and the trip to hell is over. Settling back into the body, there is much to say, for much has been noticed from that point of the Lord's companion, the device of normative behavior, the darned devil himself.

Roaring like a tiger, the little Fiona began to

strengthen her lungs. Her voice remained quiet, however, speaking through the pages, and the words and pictures in her imagination began to push and push on her blatant eagerness to spread anger on a mission, a mission to cure hell from harming, and leaving it there for hurting.

Roar. The little tiger came tumbling down Fiona's chimney and watched her. God the Father appeared as a tree stump. Then, someone cut off her foot. She smashed garlic in the middle of the kitchen with a hammer, and blood began to flow again as the stumps of her ankles curled up with her in fetal position.

Pain became negligent, as the confusion twisted around what was inside of her. Bomb squads came to intercept the many bombs that only she could detect. Every time she found one, there was one more to be found until she was so fatigued that she ran out the door to have tea with the neighbor downstairs, who called the ambulance, and not much does she remember after that.

Careful remembering brought to mind the many things she had done. Sabrina saw the opportunity to be honest with her problems and all the things she did and saw. Only no one understood.

May 11, 2005, and Fiona was admitted to a psychiatric hospital. Here is where her birthing became generative as the realities of her past pushed Heidi away like the power that launched a rocket. Speaking of rockets, while in the hospital, Fiona worked for NASA and went to the moon three times. Her strange ability to squeeze bullets from her body made her a fine warrior under gunfire. She took bullets for the ones she loved and to get to places she wanted to go. Even before the hospital Fiona had her own gun, and she protected her Mother Zebra and her Father Wolf. They looked out for her too.

In the hospital the devil gave her a pet, a wolverine that she named Wolvie, and Wolvie was careful to defend her, and Wolvie played with Korki, Heidi's old dog that had passed away.

The devil even gave Fiona a palomino stallion that was so friendly and careful with Fiona. Clip Clop was its name, and Clip Clop could even fly. Fiona rode Clip Clop twice, high in the air, and she was not afraid.

Fiona was given books from the library where Jesus hung out, and she believed beyond doubt that she had written them herself. She was just learning to read again, after the attack, the attack when hospital crew wrestled her down to the ground in a heap, after which she awakened in her "prison cell," the place where she first met the devil.

Crying voices, wailing and angry emanating from doors made her walks down the hall quite intriguing. Some rooms looked inviting, and others repelled her. The kitchen was a nice place to be during the day, but normally daytime hours were off-limits to the kitchen. There was a quiet room Fiona called the listening room that was a nice place to be as an alternative to the bedroom.

The fire alarm went off one night, and all patients had to be awakened and guided down the hall to an emergency exit that we did not use, as it was just a drill.

Just like warriors going up and down the halls, Fiona joined in the daily foot traffic that went back and forth outside of her door. Other days she sat on the footshelf in her closet and banged her feet on it, Morse code, owning that this place was her coffin and she was going straight to hell to get poisons to bring back and contaminate the world...

Satan put a stop to it right there by giving her his secret telephone number, so she could call and bleed to him instead of searching for ways to destroy the world.

What a safari. Clams, elephants, hornets, and even spiders skilled at wrapping up people populated the air of the hospitals. They were souls, not real creations, for they had never had bodies, sort of like the Holy Ghost.

These words sank to the bottom of the sea before they came out. They needed cleansing in order not to pollute the world with no repose. Miserable lechers, all those horrid and purely violent and fathoming souls seeking a body. Where does the body of suicide go? Right to the empty souls and reeking of distant thunder, a thunder of creation long ago. A suicide on the attempt of solicitude. Made to many, for many were passing through. They are gone, but we are here, some new, some old, and each in different ways.

Surrounding the newborn souls are loving hands and care and mums and pappies and brothers and sisters, grandmothers and grandfathers...not so lucky all of us. Some are born into conditions of hatred and malice, yet no child is beyond the reach of God. Every newborn child has a life already written by God. So he is not so mean, really, only onerous and unruly in the case that the world rocks and rolls, deeply satisfying to the nature of the universe.

Wrought like an egg, delicious and frothy with milky ways and delighted constellations. Faces in the sky, clearing away uncertainty that was recognized from the start as a fool sees a cow in a frog. For neither does the same for the other. We are different, far different from each other. Fiona knows. She has been visited from someone out there, out *there*. Not that we could ever go there; our egg suctions in to captivate energy, and all waste is manufactured as other stuff that uses other stuff for the prosperity of queens and kings in realms far beyond our own.

Severity accomplishes the reasons we have for being what we are. Heidi knows. She has a limit that has come to be known, and no matter how hard she pounds on the deck, her learning disorder will not go away. Still she can learn if she collaborates with Fiona, who gives her food for thought that she may never go bored. Learning ability is a lifeline to anyone who wants to maintain growth with the world. It cannot be stopped, for everybody is impressionable, no matter how motionless or disabled. A career of learning is inevitable for all people of the earth. It is a loss to cut that off, and cheating can never be right, this is known, by fact or relationship. The beauty about learning is that it brings one near to the truth. It is vowed as a waste of time and a rejection of self to cheat in the natural world. Self-encouragement keeps the mind going, and in every situation there is a place for growth in the mind and space for nourishment of the emotions.

Collaborative meaning is justice in action of naughtiness caught in the nature of very naughty naughtiness. Junk and loss and waste are never gone, only gone to subsist in a different place.

The tunnels of the universe are so vast and wide, so far and deep that I, as Fiona, belong in the hand of a human God. He is so vast and mighty that there can be no other source of protection for me in this place we call our home.

Many people keep trying and trying to change the ways of the rivers of nature. Building dams cause rivers to change their courses, and so we can act upon the universe. Even in the seasons of our earth and sun and moon there is growth and capacity changing on all our friendly planets that share this solar system. Everything seems in synch. But is this magical? We can change it. Each decision you make has a repercussion *out there.* It's violent, melodic, rhythmical. Sensations of loss and gain are flowing and ebbing with the changes of violent suicide in the earth and other fellow planets, coursing in orbit and celebrating naturally into a suicidal platitude where life grows out of cosmic significance and lucid behavior of stars and planets *out there.* So we are, right here.

MALICE AND HATRED

Anger, bitter, seething madness. An upset of all faculties as every part of the self turns in upon the self-made measurement by sheer madness. Colloquial practice as madness turns into verification of plotting vengeance. There is too much madness to plan a suicide. Vengeance is desired, yet it can't be attained. Every effort of vengeance puts you lower on the totem pole.

Why? You cry. There is so little craziness in the world and so much madness. It is so deceitful, and the hatred that goes along with it is what topples over common sense into a state of delirium.

Bitter hatred graces the toes of those who walk a road of mental illness. It is growling and irritating, and Fiona flaunts her Bengal tiger fangs. Her viciousness is an anger and an expression of the malice that would destroy the world if she could. Obviously the world is against her, but, then, why should it matter, as long as there is a God who won't let the whole world die.

Anger threatens to throttle her and irritate her madness to the point of explosion. So the bomb squad leaves, and Fiona wakes up in madness, laughing at lions in the hallways of the hospital and robots that she pushed around and swarms of friendly bees that performed a painless, perfect abortion on a rape pregnancy she thought she had.

Poor little Fiona. So little to say. Just take her pills, stand meekly in line for meals, which she always carried to her room, and laundry. She washed her own underwear every day. One day she drank water from the toilet, believing it to be holy water. Another day she took to ripping apart a book and flushing the pages down the toilet.

One day she gave Jesus a cross necklace that broke, so she gave him another one. Security made him take the necklace off, and security gave the two back to Sabrina, who became so rampant with ferocity that she stuffed them into the garbage in malicious content to curb the rage that ran through her stiffened little body. Back to the closet coffin and more Morse code.

I'm a listener, you're a singer; together we'd make a rock band. Take off your clothes and dance for the Lord, so that you can live and never be bored...

Farewell desire, for the Lord is here, and there's Mary Magdalene tugging at his ear. None so beautiful as she, she even outdid me. Oh Mary, you are so pretty.

And so on as I try to distract myself from the fury that keeps me at bay from hurting anyone. I know that when I'm this mad there's danger in hurting other people or myself, and Sabrina does not want to do that. She is a peacemaker and definitely antiwar in all she lives and breathes and does.

Carrie still cries in the dark when she's all alone, and the tower of the Lord looms high over her head, a tower that promises to protect her, not to harm her. All her life she has been quivering, sweating, crying, all curled up and sucking her right thumb. Lifeless and living alongside death, she cries now as the load above her is too large to bear. It isn't easy, and the very thing that makes her most cross is when Bertha gets cheated. When Bertha gets cheated, Carrie gets mad, and when Carrie gets mad, she begins to heal. Bertha is so innocent. Her job is to keep balanced, but the only thing she can do now is rock back and forth. Little does she know that this gentle rocking soothes Sabrina, who is insecure and must be very brave. Sabrina's key word is courage.

Even trembling she must go on. Sabrina is the flag of Dot. She is the one who is presented to the public. She shines and glows with the magic of a rainbow; only it is a circular rainbow. Sabrina loves life and puts up with the parts of her that contend to hate, hurt, kill, and anger above murder, leaving her innocent in her madness.

Anger, hatred, and weakness equal tears and struggling. Equals killing the word of schizophrenia. It is denial. The fact, the truth is that it can't be, but it is. Gory, disgusting, putrid, and malicious. Cursed, blacked out, unbearable, and given to the devil for help, who knows the ins and outs of this raging disease. So furious and grotesque, killing the soul every day that we kill a little bit of ourselves, only to be born again on the other side.

It is a cry of anger so loud that the roar is deafening through my head as the sound of hatred batters my will to try. So it takes courage. Courage to try, and that is exactly what Sabrina must do. She has no school to go to. No regular life. But that is the blessing of the illness. One must live by the rules of the illness, not the rules of the world.

Glorious, goriness, a mess of extremes that cause such confusion we can hardly fathom the pain it takes to hold it all together. Life is more than kissing death in the face, sweetly patting its back, and refusing to commit suicide. Life is for living, experiencing, breaking down, and crying interminably so hard that you're scared to leave your parents' home because an apartment isn't private enough for all the screaming you must do.

Screaming gets loud. Loud in your ears, in the room, in your soul. Fiona knows the most. Heidi has heard it, and she contains it. It funnels through her from a broken Bertha to a squashed Carrie and into a whining Fiona, who teaches Sabrina to handle pain.

Squashed Carrie yearns to go home. Rocking back and forth. Soon she will be upon a fluffy cloud of hope as hope emerges in the oncoming days of desire.

Hope is out there, but Fiona doesn't quite recognize it. She sees something more along the lines of encouragement and reinforcement. Taking a good look around, Fiona screams in silence when her little wishes are abated. What keeps Fiona going? Her imagination. She can picture what life might someday be like. She looks around and sees happiness in others and knows for her own self that she might have that someday. Also, she sees people worse off than her, so she faces the challenge of bettering herself as well.

Some people know so well how to do things, to get through life, to laugh, to have fun, to have friends, and even to know how to dance at a party. Some people know how to stand in the corner and watch, wishing, wishing that they knew how to "party." Sabrina is paranoid about the word "party." It sends her running deep inside of herself where she stays and nurtures Carrie, carefully rocking with her and soothing herself from the inside out.

"Party" reminds her of being drunk and falling all over people, usually ending up with some guy somewhere. No more. Young and frail as she is, Fiona has put restrictions on the attendance of parties. No more parties unless she feels reinforced, accepted, wanted, and loved.

No more alcohol. No more sexual harassment. No more pretending to laugh without knowing what is going on. It's embarrassing in retrospect. Mating dances with a number of different people…That is all in the past now. Painful sexual practices have led to fear of being touched inappropriately. Or being touched at all.

Fiona walks around with the big bandage of Sabrina covering her mottled and scarred appearance. Sabrina sees to it that she is a natural, good-looking woman.

Her deep emotions add to the appearance and act as an attraction that can be both a blessing and a curse. Not all the right people come and talk to Sabrina. Lonely men want to be in her company. But Sabrina walks away on Bertha's little legs.

For Sabrina, friends have come and gone. Many have turned against her, and she hears their voices in her head, taunting, misleading, laughing, ridiculing, tricking. People she thought were her friends she now counts as her enemies. People who have painfully embarrassed and humiliated her publicly, all in her head. Is it real? To Sabrina, it is very real.

Plotting, plotting against her. Constantly, the public enemy is contriving methods to trip her up. Count one, God is on her side. Public humiliation is no laughing matter. It is one of the most socially horrid feelings there is. It causes you to curse yourself until you realize that *you* are the one under attack, not the enemy. The enemy is hard to reproach. It is hard to get and has many friends.

Who is the enemy? The Antichrist. Let's not go deep into that subject; it is pretty well self-explanatory. There are many beings out there who are against the good in this world. That is the passage to safety, knowing how to navigate among these cold-shouldered idiots into the realm of heaven where we will be free of the constant danger at our backs. Always, always there is something to look out for, something evil wanting a part of you. Vices, habits, obsessions.

The dark side, the occult. Those who worship the stars, not the one who made the stars. The universe is a big eggshell, and we are birthing inside of it. I don't know how, but I don't believe we are the only ones.

Hatching eggs hurts, and a lot of pressure falls on us. Is that the truth? The crumbling walls of the universe fall down as we spread out into the great unknown where there is light all the time everywhere except when you don't want it. Magical umbrellas and powers to control our own weather systems. Magic wands and powers to cure all illnesses. So when the universe hatches, there will be the end of fear, and nature, and beauty as we know it will be as we have never known it before, in such great proportions.

Living beings will make room for all, and there will be no more death. Only defeat, defeat of the Antichrist. And he will burn in hell. There is no more to say.

Grant us freedom, oh Lord, for this promise of heaven sounds so sincere, and there is so much more to be told. The promise of total nourishment for everyone. Health beyond any we have experienced. The ability to do whatever we want, where no one will be taken for granted.

But Sabrina knows that this is only an inkling of what to expect. She also knows it is good reason to carry on as before, day to day, each day doing her best to get Dot through to the next day. Dot cannot be harmed. She is soul power.

Burning bright she shines, shines within herself, deep within Heidi, the fortress of her being. Heidi is impenetrable and lacks all social ability. Therefore people tend not to mess with her, mistaking her for a wall, or a blank, or something where there is nothing there. She lacks substance. She appears suicidal to those who reckon to see her humanity.

Heidi is frustrated beyond control. Why does this pain always come to her? Is she evil? Sometimes Sabrina believes she is evil. But to be so, she would have to be tainted by the terrors of hell. Is she evil? The point of the matter is negotiable. She is afraid of herself. Heidi can blow up any time, and she has quite a few times.

Her evil tendencies make her a good person, for she is acquainted with the enemy. She is not in herself the enemy, but she knows the enemy, and that is the key factor in being able to withstand the blows of the enemy.

The enemy is full of curses. Anger and belligerence are inserted to people as a product of the enemy. This leads to destruction, not only of others, but of the self as well. If the enemy can get us to hurt each other due to the fallen nature of our world, it is full of nasty glee. Here is how we locate the enemy, because it rises up in putrid joy, revealing itself to the world as a commonly known problem that can be attacked universally. Even disdain for the Bible is a working of the enemy. Who wants to read a book with so many details and truths, telling us that we are living the wrong ways?

Evangelism is corny and a bother. One by one people are learning to combat these misunderstandings as God works miracles in people's lives. God's miracles are powerful weapons against the enemy. Also, on a personal level, God gives us strength to do what is right and to know what is right. Most important of all, God gives us medicine out of the substances on our earth. We can heal each other as Jesus could, only through much study and practice.

Medical practice lets us live longer, more fulfilling lives. Every furthering of knowledge and practice in all fields is an evolution of our human lives as we learn to rule the earth by discovering it and ourselves. The enemy is small in this circumstance.

It can only rule backwards into history and does not understand the goodness of our future. It only understands destruction, and we won't, we can't stand for that. First of all, we have the Word, which can pass on knowledge from generation to generation. There is art to see it all as it was then and as it might someday be. Any mind totally expressed would be an awesome feature; a work beyond imagination extended as far as the limits of the mind can go or has been practiced.

The schizophrenic is processing so many ideas all at the same time for such extended periods of time that it won't do any good to try and paint all the pain and sorrow in the face of love. The enemy is incapable of love. A huge coat of armor for us.

Who is the schizophrenic? Sabrina is. So is Heidi, Fiona, Carrie, Bertha, and perfect Dot.

These personalities are all within one soul, each processing and protecting on a different level. Cookies for Bertha, milk for Carrie, sandwiches for Heidi, hamburgers for Fiona, and apple pie for Sabrina. For Dot? A banana split.

Nourishment for the soul? Nature and the Bible,

possibly church. Love for the soul, and tenderness, challenge for the mind so hope doesn't wither away from all it is and all it will do. A bright, challenging mind is further defense against the enemy, who plots statistically. The best challenge for Sabrina is to outsmart her schizophrenic illness, to take control and overcome the disease with the wit of her mind and the strength of her intellect, using her massive imagination, her talent for persuasion, and the intelligence in her cognitive glory.

Glorious pennies falling from the sky come in short amount. Now and then you find a dime, nickel, or quarter, but those are rare. Still that is not making money; it is finding money, not earned, but picked up carelessly. Thwarted once, twice, or too many times, it can be hard to find a job. There is help for people with disabilities to find vocational rehabilitation and get a job. Having a job can be highly therapeutic. It gives one a sense of meaning, usefulness, and purpose. Schizophrenics definitely qualify as disabled, and vocational rehabilitation can do wonders if the individual and the job are a good match. Working brings confidence, self-worth, happiness, and a glad heart. But it is hard to come by, to come by a match between the job and the person that will last sufficiently. Quitting job after job after job because the pressure is so great is commonly a two-month trial period for Dot, whose ideals are so very high and whose ethics believe that everyone should work to contribute to the human condition on our planet.

Each human affects another human, even if it's just to see someone that we don't want to become like. Everyone wants to better themselves, to add more to creativity, and to blind evil to the progress of mankind that we might add to our significance in the building of a world organization that drops therapy into the cups of our little ones. Smiling faces contend that something is going right. We hang out the situation and pick up eloquence along the way. Peaceably, quietly, we can all get along in the creation of malady that happens along the way when burdens fall in the wrong places. The woman in the hospital who has two days to live will remember who was kind to her and who wasn't, and this report will go straight to heaven, where everyone reads the *Silver Times,* a newspaper circulating in heaven that keeps people updated on the ongoing events of earth.

New beginnings come with changes in life. Fiona can vouch for this as she was formed out of the wit of Heidi, who normally kept things in check. Not tightly bound like Heidi, who abused every chance to be refined or glorious, Fiona was mortified at the thought of taking over Heidi's position, which she did, decapitating Heidi and spreading herself like a flower, dainty and fragrantly, beautifully surrounding the chopped-off stump of Heidi, and protecting it completely until Heidi could completely heal from the emotional trauma and stacking.

Heidi is protective of her Fiona all of the time, like the mess a batch of cookies makes when one tries to create the treat for others to have and enjoy. Digging and stacking, the rigorous trial of believing in God is enough for anyone to let futility to die in the midst of its making. The cookies are right, the song might be wrong, but all love the other when a treat is placed in front of the ugly stack. A wrap-up of personalities so coincidental that none can be seen related to one another. It is a stress case. Heidi likes to do it, to create gifts for others. She likes to be known for the good in life. She is a good wrapper. At least there was someone to bake those cookies, but Fiona didn't like to have dough in her hair, and she is naturally sloppy, so she drops the cookies and gives the chore to Heidi, who refuses to work a hand-me-down job. Not on the island of hope where we are insecure beyond severity.

Blinded by our own ignorance, there is little to hope for in this situation under the age of three. It's the little ones who know jealousy and figure out problems in traceable manners, but they work. Hit, scream, run. Hide, strike out, steal, take, use, dispose of. Once the newness runs off, there is little left to protect, and Heidi doesn't mind making a mess of things just to make revenge. How embarrassing to find your grape juice sprinkled ever so delicately over the creamy living room rug. Well exercised, totally, perfectly executed.

What is the bareness of faith in that total execution can be trusted on the field of playing kids, when Savior school principal carries you to Mommy with a twisted ankle and lots of tears. Still, there was someone there, and to make things fair, Mom and Dad are too. Carrie loves her principal; she does well in school, for nickels and dimes in report cards. The fact is, Fiona loves and always has loved to learn.

Learning is the most important ability that Heidi

shares with Fiona, and together they can be gentle and take care of Carrie and Bertha, who have suffered rape several times. Their reborn nature is to contain any contracted pain, bruises, suffering to maximum degree, and dealing with such power that pain is turned into the discipline of perfecting houses, doors, and condoms leading the rest to a place where these poor circumstances are about to become fragrant like the stink of death. Wobbling here and there, the most desperate conclusion is to open upward and turn the score over to God, so he can first take your shame, self-abuse, and denial that lead to self-bashing.

Once caring actions are interceded, healing can begin, and Heidi is strong as a healer; she churns emotions so that dirt is sifted away, and the harmless innocent, the victim carries through upon the flowery waves of hope, with magic wands of faith and belief that there is a better way. Fiona knows this. Even Curtis taught her this once.

Curtis came to her room one day, her second year at Stanford University, and conceded that he wanted to help her. Bertha, at this point totally out of her mind, connected to the people she knew and basically threw this stranger out of her room, then wept and curled up on her bed, wracked with sobs and tears that burned her sorrowful face. There was no one she could trust. Curtis would come and offer help, but his price was stiff.

"How about a back rub?"

Fiona was disgusted. Couldn't a friend be a friend without getting all physical and dangerously stupid?

It was here that the name "whore" was stuck to Heidi

in cool clothes while fluttering about like Fiona. It hurt so bad. So sickly, and to hell she went. Her head became a feeding ground for the Antichrist. Her eyes began to focus uniquely, and she lost part of her soul looking closely in the mirror. A psychiatrist tried to put her on Prozac, but Fiona, in her red, bloody uniform, could not tolerate it. She told everyone that she was tired, but her eating disorder crushed her to the point of throwing chocolate truffles and cookies down her throat, coating it all with daily frozen yogurt on her bike, until one day Fiona's bike got hit where it was located outside of her dorm. She felt helpless without that bike. Luckily, the guy at fault left a name and number, and Fiona, walking through a furnace, was restored to her fixed vehicle.

Curtis came around often, and she spit at him with her mind. She could not explain it. There was never any explanation for stupid boys who tried to get inside her mind and who gave up finally as Fiona allotted wings to herself and birthed Sabrina, who knew the only answer. *Go home. I don't fit in here,* she thought. And it was true. Her mind wouldn't function; the pills didn't seem to ease thinking. There was a big, dark block in the middle of her mind, and it was important that she get out of there before she took the stupid step: committing suicide.

Glorious hope lost with wrought of fire. All-consuming rage, Curtis in the back of her mind, leaving her behind, or it seemed Derek and Curtis paid little attention to her when she was gone. Sabrina hastily put them out of her mind, but it was not so easy to jostle them loose.

She hung on to them because it was the last connection

she had to her life plan of sanity, the journey through high school and then college and then career. No more. That plan was broken. She was broken. Her mind was broken and she could not understand it. It hurt. And soon her chest hurt. And soon her stomach hurt, tied up in knots, tighter than tight, binding and tearing, growing tighter still. There was little she could do; no one could understand this pain. Mental, physical, emotional trauma. Soon came severe anxiety. Panic attacks. Sabrina never will forget her first panic attack. Hyperventilation with darkness surrounding, her mother pulling her out of it, the terror, the horror of the creeping darkness and loss of reality.

Coming out of the panic attack left a big insecurity, knowing that it could happen again. And it did. And it has, many times, to varying degrees, each time so awful, but at least Sabrina now knows what to expect a little more. Terrible, terrible, hideous, awful, unnerving feelings that eventually pass by. Most of the time they are brought on by sensations of abandonment or loss. Feeling alone can bring on hard emotions as well. It's easy to get lost in feelings of rejection and suicide, emotional abandonment, and sensations of personal loss or failure. All these can lead to panic attacks, and they are most uncomfortable.

Suicide is a huge emotional issue to deal with. Loss of hope and final self-rejection are negative sentiments that are deplorable and lead to final failure. Most often intervention stops suicide, and, believe it or not, many times this intervention comes from God. So it did for Sabrina when she began to swallow pain pills. It was a song and then a phone call from a campus missionary that intervened in her situation. An invitation. An agreement. Sabrina put the pill bottle away.

Things didn't work out well right away. But it was as though a stone had skipped on water, the suicide issue was past. Even in her head things started to change. Sabrina depended on Heidi to get up every morning. Coffee was the one thing that could get her started, then, for a while, books took up the remainder of the day. But things got complicated. Fiona kept interfering with the reading process. She had too many things to think about, and she couldn't think and function at the same time. She tried to keep walking; this helped to process thinking out of her body and set her mind at ease.

Even in the deepest thoughts of depression, there was still room for growth, and her mind did grow. It grew to contain both normal functioning and external thinking, which was reaction to her surroundings. Fluctuating feelings were dealt with emotions and wrought with decisions. So much paranoia. Lengthy panic attacks, leaving her exhausted and terrified. Still, the days went by.

Every emotion grew. There was not much Sabrina hadn't experienced emotionally after her college years and beyond.

Feeling too much and thinking too much caused her to be slow compared to other people. She processed and processed and processed all that the world threw at her. Untimely events caught her off guard and tipped her over, careening her definition of life all over herself. She swam in the experiences of life, keeping her head up, and knowing that there had to be a way out on the other side. How ever God decided to give her a little bit of faith, it worked, and she managed to pull through every time.

Oftentimes she came through injured, broken, and missing pieces, but always having gained valuable experience to make up for it. Fair to say, many experiences were not so valuable and were rather detestable. Always sexual assault, somehow it happened. Fiona was too lazy, too trusting, too innocent, fresh meat for the kill. Not unlawful to say she had a pretty face and intriguing appeal.

Curtis came along often enough, and sometimes he could be trusted. She wanted to blurt his name to the world, only to discover that he wasn't all so interesting.

Fiasco refreshing, she hung in there and made friends with Derek, whom she stuck to like glue. It was important to have someone there to confide in, even though mental illness got in the way of social occasions, which she got used to gradually and began to enjoy to a certain extent.

Sharing wine and food at dinner with nice people was a nice thing to do. Sabrina was shy and maintained that position. She didn't get all the jokes and sometimes spoke out of turn, she forgot to answer questions…but people got used to her, and Derek liked her odd behavior.

Derek was, so to say, a real boyfriend. She loved him. She lived with him and went places with him. She thought they had a future. She was wrong. In came the dump truck and dumped Fiona Clown right into the rubbish pit. She was smothered in all the self-abuse she could muster. Drowning in self-hatred and despair. Disgust for herself, her body, her broken ego, and wretched mental illness. Hatred for her lethargic manner that sometimes took over, and anger with the olive tree that the dove found for Noah on the ark long ago. If only we didn't exist. If only there were no people. Just ghosts and spirits.

GROWING UP

Teenage experiences are difficult for everybody. Learning to care for oneself as you grow and depend less and less on other people for self-care. Responsibility is the main skill that partners into your life, and you realize that you must learn to count on you. Here is where you learn to make bad decisions and good decisions, and to deal with the consequences either way. You are the adult, the caretaker, the one who knows that you need help and you can't do everything by yourself. Discipline becomes the topic of concern, the value of belief, the route of survival.

Knowledge is necessary for the days we go through, gaining each day the respect for what we do not know, and the ability to swallow failure in a sane and palpable way. Whosoever would cancel out knowledge and lean on dreams risks failure in life where there is the need to make changes and add details to the enigma of the problem of life.

Socialization is necessary in dealing with life, because people populate our planet. We are the rulers of this world and share and trade and argue with each other. Nuisance by danger comes with greed and jealousy, where diplomacy is necessary in dealing fairly among the peoples of the world. No one is so reckless that they take without asking, and if they do, there are consequences, and war is imminent among battling childlike people of the world. That is when there is the need for want and more. Generosity is a whole different story. Some people can't understand generosity the way they do selfishness. It's a business of colloquial behavior; even in the family homes, laws of reality rule just as laws between the countries of the world.

Taking off on a sour note, we find a world with physical behavior that satisfies nothing other than the notes of reward found in the danger of reality found in imprisonment of the mind. Socialization allows the mind to deal with the mind, age to any age, sex to sex. Some people are intimidated by the differences in other people without being remotely assured that we are basically, uniquely the same inside. All of us made in the image of God.

Explosive behavior leads to shock and recklessness. Fighting, retaliation, and ultimate remorse. This is acting before thinking, reacting, and not responding; we are so insecure.

Battling leaves scars that teach us behavior. We learn to consider our feelings before we respond to certain stimuli. As Fiona grew, she was exposed to more and more pads of sandpaper. Little did she know that these were gentle cloths wiping her down after her ultimate decisions. Believe it or not, she did learn to respond, and her response was to grow. In age, in strength, in varying response, and in reply. She gave up in time of need, and she dug deep in time of need to fix her reactions into responsible replies. Teaching was the greatest return. Taking from what she'd learned and passing it onward.

Spreading her wings like a butterfly, Fiona was able to lift Heidi off the ground and flutter high in the air to visit flowers without worry. She could see, smell, and go to whatever flower she wished. She visited with bees and other butterflies. Those delicate wings carried her far and wide, even out over the waters, where she was oftentimes never seen again.

Blueberries bloom in the summer, and so do strawberries, cherries, and apples. All different, each produces a bounty of loving fruit that God has made. We are like these different fruits, and when our time of ripening comes, we provide for God a special treat by the harvest we gather among our time and talents.

Carefully groomed, each dog at the dog show is at its best, showing off not only its appearance, but its gait, its demeanor, and its attitude. Being human, we can groom ourselves and appear tops whenever we want or need to. But add to this is our produce. Progress on projects, tasks, jobs, games, chores, and all sorts of activities are unique to people. The older we get, the more highly defined are we able to complete our projects.

Little things can be important things. Even brushing the teeth. This is something you learn to do as you grow up. A paper route was the first job that Heidi had. This wasn't until the seventh grade. Her first job. Careful, and Carrie knows this, work is a tender subject for Carrie because as she grew older, as Heidi stopped the paper route, there was little left to do. She never kept a job more than four months, and that just happened twice. Always, her identity, her anonymity failed her, and fear crept into her work position, paranoia chasing her out. This mental illness, it calls for anonymity for the shame that goes with the failure it accompanies.

This schizophrenia is a mental disability, so Sabrina qualifies for government income. Enough to get by, but Fiona still wants to work, and she's dealing with the Department of Vocational Rehabilitation to try and find feasible work. A little extra money would always be a good thing. So bright eyes, open up, the future is wide; there is opportunity if Fiona will only look for it.

It's criminal to admit to a costly disability. Stigma and judgment fuel curses and behavioral candidness that is wiped dry with emotionally charged anger. The pain is hard to accept; it would rather be ignored. No one wants to admit that there is something definitely wrong with them, and when there is, such as a missing limb or malfunctioning mind, there is testimony as to why these are hard to accept. The underlying factor is fear. People don't understand. A disfigured face can be hard to look at. A missing limb can be hard not to cause staring.

Mental disabilities come in all sorts of differences. Some are externally obvious; others much harder to detect. The ability quotient is varying in degrees from case to case. Some people can't do something as simple as the laundry. Others qualify as rocket scientists but can't walk. Some people need to be spoon fed, yet make great team baseball players.

Regular people can do all things at a certain degree, no matter how minute. People helping people makes us parts of one big puzzle in this egg universe, so huge the mind cannot fathom its degree. Instruction is important in learning behavior for all people. We don't always know how to do everything all the time. We fail, fall short of our attempts, get common colds, and make a mess of our physio-psycho-animalistic powers. Medicine is so vast because the human body is so complex and because we are able to study and learn so much about it. God is not normal; he goes to extremes. We do that too, but then we break. Sickness, disease, breakage, each can lead to a limp. A limp can be respectable. Not emaciation, pallor, weakness, wheezing.

Fiona had a baby. It's a long story. And she is a princess, this she believes, and Sabrina knows. The little baby is off to adoptive parents, and her self-respect has survived because of the decision she's made in giving her to a big, loving family who can raise her well and responsibly. Fiona knew she couldn't be a single mom. She'd rather be a caring mother.

Cut off right there the story ends. She was irresponsible in getting pregnant but made the right decision. Schizophrenic voices told her to have an abortion, but her love was greater than the Antichrist.

Now there's a happy, young, little girl in the world with God's stamp on her back. Someday they will meet. Fiona will be there when Sabrina meets her daughter, when the day comes that Dot is reunited with her pristine little one.

Someday she will humble herself before this daughter, perhaps, if the little one wants to meet me. Only then will I know what it is like to have offspring of one's own. Personally, Fiona is engaged to her fiancé now for one and a half years and she has never been happier. This is Max, someone who knows Dot, but met Sabrina, and experiences mostly the acrid sense of Fiona. Fiona came out of the hospital two years ago, and she's still growing into Sabrina, with an occasional flash of Dot. Max is equilibrium. He changes as Fiona changes and is able to match her development as social circumstances push her ever forward into adulthood, walking out of arrested development.

Waking up, needing food, salt and pepper on the eggs and cheese on the sandwich, the crow flies overhead watching the eating sensation go on. Eating. Something we all have in common, even those who are fed intravenously. Food is one thing we all have in common, no matter what age. Every bite we eat grows us just that little bit more; it causes work in the body…digestion. Work causes growth, even muscle growth. Physical growth, mental growth, social growth, psychological growth, emotional growth, facial growth, hair growth, overall growth happens as we eat and sleep and work and play and time goes by.

Partying is something Heidi has been terrified of all of her existence. She's been so humiliated in social circumstances so many times that she believes people are out to get her. Heidi is just a little bit slower than other people. Slow enough to feel dumb too many times, to be victimized so many times; she trusts very little.

Max has entered Fiona's life very gently and softly. He never forced her into bed. They just sort of fell in love. Max has seen Dot and knows she exists. He has the patience of a lizard and understands Fiona in her paranoid stages, when all of life becomes too overwhelming and she enters a panic attack. He is able to talk her out of it. He treats her with so much care; they giggle and have fun together.

Heidi is broken, Fiona is squashed, and Sabrina, now, is trying to pull up the shadow for Dot. Sabrina is complicated and has lots of issues. She's afraid of Max leaving her, which he cannot comprehend. She's worried about her weight, which is a little high as a side effect to one of her medications. Not just one, but Sabrina takes six different medications to treat her illness. *Ding-dong!* A judgment factor. What do you say? Who can understand? What on earth is your right to life? It is really so humiliating; that's why it's a miracle that God brought Sabrina together with Max, who also struggles with a mental illness and takes a number of medications.

But they do help! They help keep confusion at bay, and

panic, anxiety, misery, and depression. All of which Dot has been through severely and has coated herself with several personalities to cover up her real, extra-sensitive self.

Leaping back into history, we find reasons for Fiona's abandonment issues. For most students going off to college, there is a bit of homesickness. For Heidi, there was going way off to college, far from home, among strangers where she could not socialize very adeptly, and where her mind drove itself mad trying to fit in, do homework, participate on the rowing team, and remember who she was. Heidi tried to imitate. Her homework suffered; she sought psychological help; it was so awful and painful emotionally that when she went home that summer she was diagnosed as having schizophrenia. A malady hard to understand, even harder to accept. The pain drove her mad. All mental functions shut down. She was careless and confused and stupid enough to go back down the second year. She had no other choice. In her life frame, students went to college for four years after high school, and I just must be different or something weird.

The second year was a painful mistake. More sexual victimization, the first onslaught of test anxiety, which she'd never had before.

Heidi sought psychological help and was tested several different ways. Again she was diagnosed with schizophrenia, and this time she was prescribed her first antipsychotic drugs. Whether or not or how they ever helped is debatable, but they caused immediate weight gain. Bingeing became habitual; it was painful; it was killing her. She wanted to drink a bottle of Drano.

She wanted to drown. She wanted to be attacked by terrorists as she walked around the college campus every evening. Nobody ever attacked or raped her then, out in the open. Nothing ever obvious went wrong. Her rowing performance suffered until she was placed in the last seat possible. What a blow to her confidence. One day she went for a walk with her coach, to inform him of her resignation from the team. He told her to use the toughness and finesse she'd learned in her rowing career to face the battle ahead of her. No one knew what was wrong. He said she was hard to read and could not understand her lack of gusto. What happened to the crackin,' whoppin' character who couldn't be beaten on her ground?

It was sad, and tears trickled down as she walked back to her bike to go home.

That was the last straw. Rowing was the last thing she had to hang on to. Homework was lost, concentrating in class was gone, socialization was false, and the one connection she had here was her psychiatrist, plus her connection at home with Mom and Dad on the phone and her sisters and brothers that she talked to.

Dad did come down and pick her up to bring her home during the third quarter of that second year. No one really said good-bye at all. No one must have missed her. Hell began again when they arrived home. There was one brother, Todd, and Mom and Dad and the dog. With nothing to do, Fiona burst forth into the knowledge of how to do nothing, how to fill nothing with something. Mostly with reading and drinking tea. Coffee came later. And when it came, it came hard. Todd and sister Celeste introduced her to coffee when they were all home from college. Popping like eggs in the oven, siblings came and went. There was Todd, Monty, Celeste, and Vicky. They each went to college, had vacations, visitations, and always Fiona was at home.

Monty was the oldest brother, then came Todd, then Celeste, then Dot, and last was little sister, Vicky. Dot and her siblings grew up very close to one another. They played wild childhood games at the summertime beachfront property in the woods and shared many of the same friends all through school. During young summers they engaged in elaborate games of cops and robbers, and the woods were their territory; the water was their serenity, the waves, were mattress challenges. There was a big wooden raft to swim to and dive off. There were rocks to dive off at high tide, and our parents introduced us to windsurfing that was wild fun for tan bodies in the sun.

We read books like eating candy bars with the radio on, lying on towels in the hot, tanning sun. We played badminton, all sorts of creative games in the sand, and investigative play on the oyster-covered beach below. Fishing was fun. Snorkeling lasted as long as I could bear the cold water; there was so much to see. In my younger years I wore contact lenses, and I only lost one in the sea.

Which brings me back to the glasses and braces I had to wear, glasses beginning in the third grade. Poor Carrie was tormented as the next year came around and brought braces with it for her teeth. Those lasted for four years and daunted her courage, and cheesed her smile, meaning added a frown over her grin.

Todd was very compassionate toward Carrie; he read her pain very well. He was her favorite brother, but that didn't last forever; favorites switched and ended. As years went by, Heidi felt intimidated by everybody. She was meek and childish, a little bit afraid to come out of her room.

Especially when relatives came over for dinner, Heidi, with Carrie, who was very angry at feeling differently, stayed in her room as much as possible and giggled at the table, always laughing when Mom laughed, always leaning on Mom, who cared so much.

Mom was always working in the kitchen, making the most fantastic meals, and kids were responsible to help clean up afterwards. In later years, Fiona wouldn't come out of her room at all. She came out to eat leftovers after all had left the kitchen to talk in the living room or go home. Leftovers were just as good, she surmised, but she still felt like she was barely hanging on to the bottom rung of the social ladder.

With a noose around her neck, she felt choked by her own limitations, the thoughts and feelings that kept her tied down to the bottom of the pool, trying desperately to bring up a brick, for no reasons whatsoever, except to prove that she could do it.

Fun turned into challenge. Beat yourself at what you could do. Get better and better. Then, the golden word itself: practice. If you could practice and devote time to practicing, there is just no chance that you wouldn't improve, even a tiny weensy bit.

Gaping eyes and coughing, choking, hacking roars, tearing at her body, Sabrina cried in pain with pneumonia. No one knew it was pneumonia, not until it was too late. But there was sustenance, food to bring her back. She called it Jesus soup. Jam, egg, sauce under shelf. It was a thick concoction of ingredients that was very unpalatable but nourishing. Bite by bite, prayer by prayer, the soup went down, and suddenly bread and carrots looked good again. Like a donkey down the road, that carrot looks good, but you can't have it until you've done the work to get to it. The Jesus soup whet her appetite enough to make regular food possible to keep down, or even to get down.

Who knows if it was pneumonia? Could it have been malaria? The possibility is there. Somehow, somewhere along the line, Dorothy died and became Dot, a pruned and trimmed version of the original. She cast her soul to heaven, and it came back rent in two, filling her body with the power of one. One that could talk like two. Two that could talk to each other. It was a growing-up experience for a case that no doctor could ever seem to diagnose until she was labeled with schizophrenia…this long before Jesus soup, way back before she moved out of her parents' the time after college, into a room for rent that worked out excellently with housemates.

Of course, lonely, longing Heidi, Fiona wanted to be closer to Curtis, so when the studio opened up, she moved in across the hall from him and away from the new friends she'd made at the house with the job at the violin shop.

Things were going well, until Fiona dismissed Heidi and beckoned Sabrina in, not knowing that she'd become codependent, a word she learned later on in life after a painful separation from Curtis who said they were just not compatible.

Fiona looked and looked and looked for a job but felt she had nothing to offer. It was subtle at first, but schizophrenia came ringing through after about a week of exposure to any new situation. Sad and specific, crying with shame, the border lines were clear. She clearly could not deal with the public. She was still learning to deal with herself, how sometimes she let herself down, tricked herself into doing things she regretted, and ran from situations that appeared intimidating.

She got confused, forgot instructions, performed the wrong tasks, and allowed money to slip out of her hands at the cash register. How shameful. To be counted dead among the money dealers with fumbling fingers and crooked math sketches in her head.

Numbers appeared menacing, even after all the training she'd had, how well she'd performed in that subject. Foreign language was another subject that came quite easily. Now forgotten, there are bits and pieces that jump up here and there. To remember what you've forgotten is a brand new discovery. It is enlightenment that reminds you that you are smart after all, despite all the muddle and fuddle that remains out of all the school learning you've had. Sabrina is quite intelligent, bright, energetic, and quivering with imagination. She is in self- denial and causes her self-esteem to remain flat and trampled upon. Not many people could have gotten as far as she has, but she has had unconditional love from her family and from God. So she may not know it, but her self-belief is below her self-denial, meaning she can't give up on life.

Loss of confidence grows greater and higher as self-doubt expands lower and wider. Changes come quickly and suddenly or slowly and dubiously. One reason to keep going through all the hoops is the love of conquest when discovery of self-ability is applied through appearance.

Dot has found meaning in life, and this keeps her getting out of bed each morning, tending to a structured day, and using creativity to bring a sense of clarity to the lights in her mind. Landing in the life work of appearance is the ability to separate life from the confusion of disconcerting eloquence. She needs to appear as herself and loathes the idea of becoming a carbon copy. She's learned that this road is too painful. It is best not to compare oneself to others. You are too useful as you are, and that is best.

Putting up a front, in other words, is the wall that hides Sabrina from Dot, the beautiful princess who has found Max, her prince. Only the stages are preliminary, and neither knows the other truly, not yet, except to shoot out to the stars and write in the starry glow the words "soul mates."

Lucky or not, there is luck in the world, and Fiona has found a bit of it for you. There are changes and consequences, subliminal happenstances, and measurements of insecurities where tears pour out in numbers unfailing, but good things seem to happen in the end.

When does unfailing come through as though there were no such thing as trust and anxiety? Faulty or not, there is a measurement of truth that fills vast mountains of doubting minds with the doubt that leads to violence, even violence turned on the self. Pleasure in itself is not necessary to express in numbers the very need of self-explanatory behavior, for there are eggs in every female, and trails to lead them to expository induction. Where the landing falls is rather scientific, leading us on to realize that there is little to know what really takes care of the numbers nonending.

Very far from the future is the present; in fact, each is split by a cord of infinity. A beautiful columbine of creeping, crawling flowers and affectionate kittens rolling around in balls of yarn. Where play is work is when goodness becomes violence or abuse. When enough is enough. Sometimes that is hard to identify, for when good is good you don't want it to leave, and denial sets in for the singular idea of discomfiture that suddenly leaves a division between mentally enjoyed pleasure and physical/emotional sedition. Everyone experiences loss of a good thing, but if you have hope, you can believe that goodness will come by again. Hope is the magic trust, the feeling and belief that keeps us trying, knowing that life can repeat itself in new and different ways.

Far from beauty, Fiona begins to break down as the

fight for pleasure to hang on grows deeper and deeper imbedded into her psyche. Flailing about, it is as though her two feet are cut off and the blood pours forth. Overnight they are returned but to be treated not with the ultimate respect. Feet are the most important part of Fiona's body image. It is with her feet that she can outrun her perpetrators. The ugliness of sin and grueling sex and ugly brainwashing in the wrong churches. The ability to flee is her prized ability and to kick and thrash violently when caught is another powerful defense mechanism.

What a sad topic. A wild animal should never be caged, but God gave man this planet and all its life to manage and subdue. If ever the lion will lie with the lamb, then violence must be conquered through positive violence.

Curative strategies let us know that there is little we can do in the midst of torment, especially when alone. There is power in numbers, and in numbers we shall overcome. Communicating faster and faster over farther and farther distances is speeding up our ability to surprise attack and counter the enemy. Nothing short of violence if diplomacy can be successful and everyone's wishes made known.

In a way we all grow up, kids keeping our childhood values and dealing among each other with the same ethics taught to us long ago, instilled in us as part of our human genetic makeup. All humans are made to act like humans. We further our sciences, our societies, our governments, and even our prison systems. There is always hope if we follow and change the rules dealt by the majority of the earth's population.

The earth turns, and every rotation brings a new day. Work, work is what keeps us going and growing. The more the earth matures, the more we have learned about it and can utilize all it has to offer. People give their lives making discoveries. Funerals happen in order of death. Death is a part of life. According to Jesus, we can rise again into a place called heaven, so not to worry.

AMBUSH

After Fiona moved in across the hall from Derek, she started spending more and more time over there. She clung to him like glue. It was real codependent behavior. Both were in need of the other, and it was a love relationship that lasted for three magical years, other than the intruding bother of Sabrina's mental illness. It was something Derek learned to accept and put up with, considering the positives on the other end of her personality. He kept her laughing; she kept his ego shined and polished. Together they would go out to restaurants with friends from Derek's work and his family. Sabrina's family never really took to Derek. He was too high strung. He was a talented musician, and Dot, being quiet, sometimes came out to enjoy the web of

classical guitar music that flowed through his apartment.
She knew when he saw her; there was a glow in his eyes,
and she disappeared just as fast from her reverie, back into
the book she happened to be reading, just good old Fiona
who loved to bother Derek for attention...

Derek was very eager to show off his prize Sabrina,
who said very little but smiled and looked pretty. It
wouldn't work out. Too much pressure on Sabrina to do
this, to do that. Then came the night of the ambush. It
was after dark, and the two were driving home from a
concert. Derek pulled over at a viewpoint, and Sabrina
mulled over the speed of society as they watched the cars
racing back and forth across the I-90 bridge. So fast.
Everyone in such a hurry. Derek seemed about to say
something but changed his mind. It was over just like
that. As they waited at the intersection to the main road,
a man came and knocked on Derek's window, seeking
money. "*No!*" Sabrina cried, her instincts flared to one
hundred degrees. As she reached to help him, her own
lights went out with a big thud, the boom as something
hit her head from her side of the car. A setup, an ambush.
Groggy feeling and dizzy, she lay back in her seat, and as
the cars went by, her lights went out.

Dazed, later, she was counting fingers to see the damage
done. Four seemed like three, and two seemed like three.
Ugly visions danced across her eyes in a strange reverie,
as dogs came up and slowly licked her feet, her hands,
and her face. They rolled her over, and she coughed up
blood. A strange sickness caused nausea to rule over her

body. She wobbled back and forth in her bed, and the sickness brought vomiting, which brought relief.

Strange pseudo-science clarified the mischief more clearly than the offense. Biotic means of behavior must have cost her millions of dollars in thought. Thought blockage, enraged behavior, learning to walk again. But where was everybody in all of this? Was she to save her own life? Here came Jesus soup. Here came toe by toe, foot by foot, sitting down throughout the exercise. Didn't anyone know she was fighting paralysis, starvation, and loss of thinking ability all at the same time? She would not become a lost patient. She would fight to the finish, even when this meant losing Derek, whose codependent behavior was based on cocaine in the coffee anyway.

This was no laughing matter and had two sides to its nature. First of all, Derek used a mild dose of cocaine in the coffee every morning, and this kept Sabrina hooked on and happy; no wonder she loved her coffee so much. The other side looked happy, because this magical coffee is what helped her endure some of the more difficult seasons of her illness.

"I don't think I could have made it through," she reasoned in later years when all was found out. None of this had ever been known to Fiona, let alone Sabrina. Apparently she'd uncovered a drug circulation with her crazy antics and knack for getting into the middle of things without invitation.

Good fortune, good luck, bad luck, there is this blockage in her head due to the ambush incident. Luckily, all other faculties are intact other than a certain clumsiness in getting around. But this can be learned, and then all is well that ends well.

When she had a paper route in the seventh grade, Carrie and Bertha used to walk the streets of her neighborhood and deliver newspapers. Carrie and Bertha used to go door-to-door collecting one dollar from each house each month. All tips were for keeps, on top of fifty dollars.

Back then it was a modest collection for a first-time job. For a seventh-grader. When Bertha went to sleep, Carrie finished eighth grade waking up Heidi Clown, who blinked her eyes and looked around at this strange new world. Carrie knew she was too small to handle high school, and soon enough, Heidi swallowed her up. What does this have to do with anything? It just shows that people adapt. They have to adapt to the strange situations around them that God throws at them by altering their personalities in order to be able to deal with them in a peaceable manner, and peace is of utmost importance.

Waves upon the ocean shore, wind among the branches of the highest trees, snow falling softly over icy lakes, and sun rising quietly over rippled waters. These are peaceful scenes and places Heidi can go when all other thoughts have strangled a noose around Fiona and Sabrina, backfiring, retarding her development to the moments of her high school era.

There is a skip and a jump and manners come into play. A vision, a force, and maniacal thoughts about dogs dying in the road play softly across her face as she plays softly against the ropes that tie her down. Very vigilant is the man who watches over her and raises his voice as she strives to get better on her own. It is that old grandpa, the one who swatted and betrayed her with a paddle in her own room. The truth was too ugly, so she made up that one. It wasn't true. Grandpa never did anything, but let's just say he did, for the sake of insult upon hurt.

Blocked out now was anything she'd learned about social etiquette, and that was not very much, which is disconcerting when one learns how lonesome Sabrina has been for most of her life, if she includes her multiple personality. She dare not look at Dot, not wanting to ruin her precious life.

Symbolic, not eclectic, are the ways of her ruined household. Celeste moved away a long time ago, and Vicky was not far to follow. Monty was the first to leave and to become financially successful, having crossed continents and foreign language to raise a somewhat dysfunctional family there. Todd hung around home for much too long. He claimed that there was nothing wrong with Fiona. He could not acknowledge Fiona's mental illness, and he taxed her with harmful opinions and radical assault. Todd was special to Fiona but rejected that fate in time of horror as she curtsied her way away from the disco freak he had become to her.

There was nothing she could do, for her opinions were never strong enough to match his overtones, and had he not been the one to save her life one cold Christmas, she would have rejected him completely. As it was, she forgave his misbehavior until she realized it would not stop. It drove her crazy. It drove her mad and into the hospital, where she couldn't help but think that all men should continually masturbate or else cut their penis off.

Rectal penetration was going a little too far, and her mind, as small as Bertha's in a socially adept Sabrina mind frame could not pump up enough stereo to climax the disgusting behavior that went on day after day. Too weak to admit to the wrong, Heidi was the only one strong enough to be courageous enough to turn the story around and begin to fight back. And she did. With mad passion and aggravation she tore into the hospital attendants as they struggled her to the floor. That was all she could remember, except for the spider web that wrapped up her previous boyfriend, who said he would help but never did.

She remembered laughing hysterically for hour after hour, exhausting herself, yet unable to stop; everything was so funny, so extremely funny. Even elephants made it onto the raft that would exit this planet and go on to the next one, where paradise would be forever more, not for those left behind. Every creature came, even anteaters, which would take care of the only problem left, the ants, which would sneak aboard uninvited.

Sabrina woke up one day and realized she was pregnant. All four babies were stillborn before birth, and hornets came to clean out her uterus as the most carefully skilled insect on the planet to take care of the procedure.

They even cleaned up the mess. Sabrina got pregnant again, and in three years she would give birth. Time was different up here. Up here on Saturn.

She would never age past thirty-six, and all men

wouldn't age past thirty-seven. So her children aged as she gained maturity without aging. Sabrina had three children, Tiger, Pipin, and Daria. All three grew up to work in the hospital where Sabrina lived, was given daily care and comfort.

It was beautiful here, and even though she stayed inside the walls of the hospital, the windows afforded a view so rapturous that heaven felt like a soft sponge on an inkwell. Here she grew, there she threw, and fell, and ran, and made fun, always hurting her head somehow. By straining past her limits, she began detecting bombs and the CIA and the FBI and a belief that the two were at each other's throats.

Sabrina saw ghosts and robots and rich, famous men who got locked up to die without food or water.

Then came her court date. And the story goes on. Sabrina was ousted from this fun, safe hospital down to another not-so-fun safe hospital where she stayed one more month before being set free. Taking one thing with her, a new pair of glasses that came three weeks late, which was probably a godsend. Five and a half months without glasses was total mind therapy. It allowed her to focus on the aura of the individuals around her and the one she was talking to, not the exact features. It's hard to explain…

What a loser. What a reject. Yet people still seemed to love her, to like her, and she took care of herself. Relearned shopping, scheduling counseling appointments and keeping them, walking, eating well, and crying now and then. It took time for Sabrina to adjust to independent life outside of the hospital, in her own home, the happy condo where she lived with her three cats.

Todd bothered her. She didn't know why and couldn't stop to think of a good reason, not for a few years later.

Both Todd and Monty came to visit in the hospital.

Vicky got married that summer, and Sabrina wasn't told about it; it would've broken her heart not to be there. Celeste had her baby boy, the first of her sisters to give birth. Sabrina loved her brothers and sisters; they knew her from childhood and all the family secrets she shared with them.

But Sabrina was sad. She was a loser. She'd lost her daughter, for a long time her pride and self-respect, her ability to communicate. English was her first half language. Then there was gesticulating and word searching until her meaning was made clear. She'd lost all confidence and self-esteem. No more belief in herself and, less than ever, a shortage of hideous mind control. There were all thoughts of the Antichrist in her mind, countered by images of God and blood and her feet being chopped off. She whined and whimpered. It was a savage blow, this experiment with going off of her antipsychotic medicines.

They saved her life, as she was rounded up and escorted to the hospital for urgent care that spring when dandelions became the remedy she thought would be the cure. It was hopeless, merciless, painful, and discouraging, the beginning and the end all at once.

She hated herself, hated life, cursed God, pulled stickers out of Jesus and prodded him over and over again, until she was made known that he was her friend, and the stickers weren't really painful anyway. Just like the gentle reed that Jesus would never break, he would never break Fiona, and this made her angry. She wanted to be punished, to be proved that she was a whore, that nobody loved her and her curses were blessings that wrapped around each other to bear tidings of abhorrent language pouring from her mouth. Dirt language that no one should have to listen to, so she mindlessly kept it to her quivering whispers and mulling words that sounded senseless.

Round and round she went killing people with her mind, knowing that they did not exist anymore in her imagination. She made up stories to explain away her behavior, her rambunctious attitude toward God. That fiend who said she hated God was quite easily disposed of as her heart melted in the tenderness of his loving care. Even in a wheelchair he could love her with a lion's heart and the strength of the father of all lions.

Uncoordinated and let down, time after time, Fiona began to realize that this powerful God was on her side. He fought for Fiona through a barrage of people that Sabrina felt unable to mention due to the highly secretive nature of his workings in the universe. According to the Bible, there was allotted hope for those who loved him.

Carrie remembered him as a small child in Sunday school. She remembered her very first Bible that she disposed of angrily after becoming mentally ill. How could a loving God do this to her? She was vehement, and that Bible, with her name engraved, was sent to the dump via the household garbage can.

Fiona felt a twinge of guilt.

That Bible flew away on wings of ownership and returned to Fiona many years later in the form of another Bible that came to her through her Friday night University Christian Fellowship group. This time Fiona was in trouble. She knew she needed help. She was taught how to pray, and when someone prayed for her for the first time, she felt a twinge of magic...or love. This time she kept the Bible and read it front to back, becoming more and more devoted as the pages turned and applied themselves to her battered life.

More beaten down, Fiona tried to fit into this Christian group. She attended Friday night worship and study, which was all fine until the time came to be social. Poor Fiona sat in her chair and looked around futilely, hoping someone would talk to her, and a few people took an interest. A fleeting interest. Every time she drove home depressed, let down, hurting, blaming herself, and wanting to die. She felt like a great big clown. One night she stopped in front of her old high school and screamed and screamed until she might choke. Gasping, gagging, her perplexed form drove home to Mom and Dad's house where she took her pills and dove into bed, hugging herself in a curled-up ball.

Fiona had no better luck when she tried going on weekend retreats with the group. All she wanted was to remain hidden, and that seemed to be impossible. There was mealtime, worship, and game time, which

Fiona avoided, staked out in her room with her Bible. The game for her was to get sustenance, make limited contact, participate in small groups, and to disappear when it came time to do skits.

She much more enjoyed the planned teaching, when guest speakers took their turns. Fiona did what is called dissociation during these weekend retreats and hid herself inside of herself, expressing reaction, reflection, and imposition rather than response. She hid herself completely, faked who she was, and acted out a personality based on what she'd seen in Celeste and Vicky in the growing-up years. She smuggled herself onto the van at departure and felt weak and disliked, rejected, a bother. She cried again and again as her fake happiness wore off and it was back to scar-flecked Fiona. She cried and cried until her soul was torn open. Not always with tears.

Faking happiness just proved her clown-like behavior. Maybe she laughed too much or giggled too profusely. It was her heart that hurt the most. Such a clown. No one could decipher her attitude; her camouflage was practiced to the point of expertise. Her escape routes were mapped out to a tee.

She could disappear at the drop of a dime and always show up on time for transportation and meals. She learned to pray; skeptical and desperate, she ended up spending hours in prayer, especially while consuming Jesus soup. Each bite was an eternity, and each bite required prayer, so far as peace in Iraq, and financial ease for herself throughout life. Prayer contaminated her opinion about everything. It helped us realize that there was a hope and a mind in the strength of character behind the ever-shifting personalities of Dot.

Once Jesus soup was almost gone, Dot got to eat carrots and bread. It was a miracle forsaken, as Dot came out of hiding a little bit and began to sit down and write about her troubles. Dot emerged again on the piano, but this was all briefly, because Derek dumped her when she went off her medications and subsequently went out of control. Dot ducked and hid before she got her head cut off. Yet, she survived, deep in her soul. She never had to fake herself again. Sad eyes and demeanor. She continued on in life, as Fiona registered with the local mental health center where she got help and a focal point to swing around as her life began to grow and develop.

Growing and developing entailed learning how to socialize, how to grocery shop, how to go to the bank, the post office, and to pick out clothes that she liked and that fit her seasonally. It meant keeping busy and reading a lot, going to church, staying in touch with family, and dealing with family and friends as strange relationships developed. Clowning around can only explain the harassing voices in her head as Fiona and Sabrina learned to deal with life.

The conspiracy against her was most disturbing and ate away at her position in life. She cursed the voices, battled with them, and tried to destroy them using the blood of Jesus. Her cats kept her calm and company. She felt destructive and wanted to break things. She was hospitalized at least three times, once going loony after the birth of her child.

There was so much pain in this area; it dulled her senses and grounded her mind into the earth, letting the healing touch of nature do her trick by using logic to prove she'd done the right thing by adopting her daughter out.

Birth control became necessary, so Fiona chose the IUD. She didn't need it. She stopped flaunting her body for attention. When Fiona met Max, she needed Sabrina to help her open up to him socially. Soon the two were dating, and Max, his mind made up, decided to have a vasectomy done to ensure no children. They met at the mental health center, each with a mental illness, and a lot in common.

Dot was schizophrenic, and Max was schizoaffective. The two were complimentary conditions and made Max and Sabrina likely partners. They kissed first on New Year's Eve and became engaged June first. Nearly two years later they've been through a lot together. Discovering each other's strengths and weaknesses.

Sabrina had her IUD removed. She didn't need it anyway, not with Max being her one and only, and that he was. This was true love, something she'd experienced only mildly in high school, and now it was happening slowly to her. It wasn't all fun and games, but there were bridges to cross and seas to swim. With initial timidity and growing confidence, Dot moved slowly to Max, as he slowly let her know who he was. Love was something far from her immediate vocabulary, romantic love. The love between a woman and a man. She could hardly believe what she was getting into. The fact that there was no abuse, no horny gentleman who hoodwinked her and said good-bye.

Such sadness flowed from her insides that she could hardly contain the love that replaced it as it was nurtured slowly away. Trust was a huge fondling issue, a concern that became a relaxing factor as each turn provided truth and admittance of good behavior. This was no skeleton. No creep, sleaze, or slimeball. This was Max. A daunting creature, a soulful man made of justice and innocence, also plagued with a mental illness and bound by the love in his heart for Dot and all her personalities. Understanding was the greatest gift he could give. Not ridicule or abhorrence. He took her in for who she was. A beautiful, stately princess of the Lord.

This shone with everything she did. Demure, saintly, quietly, respectful. With a heart of love and shining glory in everything she touched. Sabrina was very observant. Observant of others and of herself as well. For years she observed her behavior, even before her clownish behavior came along. Heidi merging into Fiona was a total time of observance and analytical behavior.

She mocked herself, made fun of herself, and purposefully put herself into embarrassing situations, completely a clown of mirth; her heart was torn with sadness and depression. Depression led a life of its own. It killed from the inside out, slowly chewing on all her bright ideas and casting them away as unfit and untidy, not right for this world, too laughable, too clownish, and unbelievable.

Her mental illness backed this up and left a drop-off, where reaching for her goals meant stepping forward into disability, and falling, falling into the depths of reality.

Limitations, those awful, frightening limitations that seemed to pop up everywhere as she got to know herself and the scope of her illness. Abhorrent, abhorrent disaster, pain, loss of self-respect, and sadness that covered over everything. Everything in and out. Up and down, over and under, side to side.

You can't escape it. The frightening confusion of inability and disability, where one slides and the other tapers off.

A fighting chance to recover is available if one learns to work with the illness and not against it. Dot's anger at herself for having these limitations spoiled her impression of others, and she hid behind Fiona, of all clowns, to make sure that she knew herself before letting herself be known. Here it is a dinosaur, for the deeper you go, the older you get, without aging. This comes by reading books and studying what it was like long ago, and then applying that to your own life. Then it's not so hard to stand still. Floating possibilities keep you trying, because every time you catch a fish, you have reason to believe there might be another. We can't believe in the future, but in a pattern of change and repetition. It's a delight to kiss the world good-bye and go along your own way, acknowledging and recognizing without meeting and greeting.

The favorite part of being a clown is that nobody really knows exactly how you feel except other clowns. The secret to being a clown calls on a long history of feeling disliked, discarded, and ridiculed. Clammed up and realized to yourself as a jewel yet undiscovered.

Clowns speak a different language. Part body language.

Part language of habit. Part surface communication. And then the language of emotion, guilt, upset, steady laughter, sleep, weight gain, raised voices in anger, disbelief, blame, self-blame, buddy-buddy, understanding, falsehood, leading on, letting go, meanness, pride, poor me, self-hatred, and more. These are communication skills that are abnormal, having left out the most dominant, silence, whimpering, tears.

Scalding tears stay flecked on my glasses, needing to be washed three to five times a day. That much time in grief, it's unbelievable. Horrible, relieving in a way, just as relieving it's been to start walking in circles, pacing back and forth, sitting down and swaying from side to side, having unnatural leg movements, and lots of holding her head in her hands, to rest the weary center of all this confusion.

All clowns are confused. They don't know whether to laugh or cry, and then, when doing one or the other, fear that the expression of that emotion is improper. Unfocused, cloudy thinking, and a heavy dependency on coffee for enjoyment, plus to relieve some sedating effects of the medications that Dot has to take.

Medication is a huge issue that we don't have to discuss right now. In the meantime, there are food issues, to friendship issues, to educational issues, and even self-care issues, such as acknowledging that she has the mental illness, and agreeing to see a psychiatrist regularly who prescribes medications, and a case manager who deals with social issues, such as housing, occupations, treatment, such as art therapy or other interactive group settings.

The "consumer," or mentally ill individual, has a role to play. To engage in therapy and be active in recovery. Mental health professionals can do all they can do, but unless the consumer takes part, little headway can be made.

Sabrina took part from the very beginning by seeking help voluntarily at Stanford as a wracked, individual freshman unable to fit in or complete assignments. She sought help in the psychology department, not knowing where else to go. She never learned the word "schizophrenia" until her second year at college, when an immanent recovery did not occur, like her recovery from mononucleosis had been. This pain stayed on. The confusion, the laughter, the not fitting in, the fright caused by other people, the schiz-schiz-schizophrenia! Now to discover what it meant. If I knew then what I know now, I most likely wouldn't have made it through the bargain of life.

That summer was so confusing. Sabrina tried to coach adult novice crew. She did it, by what power she knew not, but her ratings were very low. Most of them read "too quiet." For assistant coach she did okay, except for nearly driving her launch into an innocent beginning windsurfer. It was a close call. Luckily, the near accident was fairly unnoticed.

Flames of voices killed her spirit that year. Sweat and mononucleosis. Ghosts everywhere, her angel, Gabriel, revealing himself as a reflection in a shop window. Jesus walking her home from a bus stop where she'd nearly exploded into total outward psychosis.

Always that time bomb ticking away inside of herself. Pitiful, disgusting. Coffee guzzling and book after book. Coffee shops where Fiona would make journal entries, private and powerful. She went everywhere with a notebook and pen. It was therapy. Both computer journal writing and written journals. Words. Words, words, words. Jesus is the Word. So it says in the Bible. Oh, that Bible. So much to learn and reiterate, to blow out of proportion, only to magnify what comes next. Rippling around and creating patterns consistent in and throughout.

Whirlwind carrying me through life, personalities and all. It changes meditation patterns and signifies gentle measures used to treat the self, especially when one comes down to the line and wants to hurt herself. Magnified damage is implicit in coordinating the ultimate reproach considering danger and harm. Self-defense against self lies in a belief that there is love, and nothing much matters after that. Every baby was loved at one point and carries that memory through life, no matter how distant or well buried. God is love, is love, gives love, and takes love away. The awesome experience of falling in love is a replacement for lost love that leaves a tracing for new love to follow.

Following ultimately leads to leading, and surely enough, those who have experienced the most hatred provide the greatest of leaders, for they understand the policy of want and need. The pressure is revoked when a little love is sprinkled to light the way. And what is the way? Where are we headed? It takes a lot of love to figure that one out. First, we have to believe that we are worth saving. That's questionable as we look at hatred, malice, and harm done everywhere.

Sabrina has found that it pays to take a good look at the self, what is left of it after damage done. Get to know the self and study others. Here we are, all created the same, but totally different in presentation. Each individual is structured totally uniquely and fashioned after the same human pattern that began with Adam and Eve.

From the beginning, into the sunset we whistle as the winds go by, angels of the Lord, for the one who was crucified to signify the meaning of love unto death and forgiveness.

Crude people we are, compared to the finesse of Christ, who could obey his Father's will in order to set the people free of distrust among all, if we begin to examine ourselves in the light that he lit long ago. It is an example that need not be repeated, a comfort to all, who could turn and follow. Sabrina believes that this is the way, this is who we should follow, who will lead us onward if we consider and imitate the examples of teaching, instructing, and performing.

Acting, responding is one thing that Bertha, Carrie, Heidi, Fiona, and, for some part, Sabrina, could not do. Their basic nature was to react immediately to whatever came their way. They could react but not respond. They could relate but not interrelate. It was a stuffed-up closet of emotional garbage and refuse from rotten thoughts not communicated. Stuffed behind a wall of false reality.

It took a huge calamity for Sabrina to learn responsibility. Her growing up years were a chocolate cookie always waiting to be eaten. Always dodging danger and mixing up a new batch before the last was eaten. Sweet reality that was all but manufactured and tended with a magic wand that only worked sometimes.

Flat face, disfigured, manufactured elements of surprise, forgotten thesis of sauerkraut on top of the head, to temper too much sweetness that caused people to have a bellyache of disbelief and revolt. Rotten sweetness in Sabrina began to stink as she began to realize that nothing about her personality was real, except the many flowing tears and clownish grins and giggles.

She struggled with words to make herself known, and finally, with an explosion as great as a busted dam, the words began flowing out of her in sickening waves of authority and danger. She was near the edge when Curtis caught her and pulled her away.

Sabrina left this young man for her mother and father's home, where she slowly began to discover herself.

She trusted no one. She didn't trust her pills, but Vicki gently goaded her into taking them again, so she did, and they helped matters a great deal. Dot had been schizophrenic for nearly ten years by now and had gone through a gargantuan ordeal of living with this disease. It was not clownish. It produced clowns.

Clowns dance and tease and play and hate and love and do lots and lots of tricks to make people scared and to laugh. But clowns get to go home and strip off all that makeup and funky clothing to turn into comfortable street clothes and become a regular individual. Sabrina didn't have a job, so she did what she wanted. She read books, went for walks, and spent a lot of time thinking. This was primary. Then there was hospital diversion group to go to and become accountable at the mental health center and art therapy to exercise creativity.

There was friendship practice, and Sabrina had friends, distant and close; the more honest she was, the more real the friendship.

Heidi never really had a friend, Fiona had fake friends who turned against her in later life, and Sabrina finally began to ascertain who was and who wasn't a true friend. Dogs make good friends.

Suddenly, Sabrina realized that she, herself, made a good friend. This came through a realization that she'd carried a good friend with her all those last fifteen years that she'd battled with her mental illness, a process that was beginning to become habitual, yet struck newly every time an onset came bashing into herself, and voices took over in her head, breaking bonds of trust, yet no longer could they totally break her. Max understood; he had voices too and more often. It was a terrible dilemma, but at last Max and Dot had each other. There was nothing to lose there. The combination was perfect, and two could hold each other up through all sorts of storm and hail and lightning and deafening thunder.

Breakups were hurtful, and there weren't many, as Sabrina never got close to many people. It was hard to reveal the truth about her illness to anybody, shameful and unrepentant she felt. Forgiven for everything, she blamed herself for everything, large and small. No two ends could meet, yet Dot and Max clapped together to the same tune at the same rhythm. No one met them really; they had a private life and began searching out faith in the Catholic Church.

There was no ambush here. Although there were visions and voices that tormented them individually, no one dared to trip them up. It was aquatic in a way, waves of good and bad days, and good and bad within days, sometimes durations of weeks, always teaching lessons on how to better handle the illnesses.

Sometimes they met sharks, like unexpected bills, and jellyfish, like milk gone bad too soon. Beautiful visions on sunny days as they walked hand in hand a good three miles around the neighborhood was good for exercise and strength in dealing with the illnesses. Employment came and went. Sabrina did some volunteering at the local hospital and is currently seeking volunteer employment at the local library. Sabrina loves books; they light her up like a fire.

Words are fascinating. They communicate from one to another, and books can be read by millions to understand the same message. It's amazing how all the different languages can say the same thing in a different way.

Music, too, is one of Sabrina's passions. In fact, today she complains about her hearing, having listened to very loud music for years in order to block out hideous voices and maddening emotions. Only occasionally does she turn it up now.

Sabrina used to play the piano well, but not anymore. Her fingers have lost their touch, or some connection has been broken in her mind. This is sad, as music was such an escape for her, especially when she lived by Derek.

She taught herself and learned quite well, but then came the ambush that dark and cursed night when their car was attacked from both sides at a dark intersection, and the two of them were assaulted, as far as she can remember, losing consciousness, and that was the end.

CLOWNS

Can you wake up in the morning without remembering the night before? Yes? It's very possible, especially if you are drunken and reeking of vomit, not knowing how you got back to your own bed. What an awful feeling as you feel between your legs and they're wet and full of germs. Gross. First thing to do is take a cold shower and then turn it hot. Icky nut heads. Men seem to be attracted to that one spot, and spoiled women are apt to give it up, over and over and over again. It's sad, pitiful, to blink your eyes and realize you can't communicate your feelings to anybody. You just can't talk without faking it, without playing the clown.

Nobody knows how many men have raped you, and how many times you've let yourself be had for fear of rejection, and then you are rejected and humiliated anyway. Beasts, they are. Hungry, roving, college-party men who sucker innocent women into their folds. For a roll in the hay, dirty enough to say, and then a weak apology for spoiled friendship ruined like a sunken ship.

Fiona lost her focus. Despite her mental illness, which she had not yet acknowledged, she tried to go to her classes and attempted homework assignments. She felt revolting and repulsive to her roommate, whose two best friends lived down the hall. She felt boring, ugly, her clothes were gross, and she was getting fat from her antipsychotic pills. It was hellish. She tried to hang around with them but felt so boring and ugly that in the end she chose to hang out by herself.

Fiona's fake friends from her first year of college came around only once, and she lost touch with her crew teammates after quitting the team with loss of hope and drive. She could no longer serve the team and was so humiliated, having gone from first to last seat in the boats, being unable to keep up on land workouts; it was hopeless, and she refrained from carrying on.

People asked her what she was going to do. *What do you mean?* she thought to herself. Couldn't she just open books and look at them and underline sentences, pretending to study and write enigmatic papers that barely missed the mark of the assignment? She followed her German teacher downstairs after class one day to ask him not to pick on her so much, and he was merciless. No one understood. She followed a philosophy teacher downstairs once after class and whispered to him,

"What is imagination?" Yet he did not hear her shy, quiet voice, and she dared not repeat herself. She asked an anthropology group leader the meaning of the word "concept," and many people laughed, but the question never got answered.

She asked a computer professor if the class was hard. His answer made sense. "It depends on how much work you put into it," he'd said. Computer class was significant. It met twice a week, and after class on those two days she allowed herself to go tanning. This was a paradise, dream getaway. So was the bookstore just across the street.

Her one "A" she got in piano class, but she felt frustrated, as if she wasn't learning anything. It did feel good, however, when the class applauded her after she played her final test piece at the end of the quarter. She felt appreciated, approved of. It was her only positive affirmation.

Deep, deep into the depths we go. Howling and shrieks beginning to bubble up inside. Forty-five-minute showers. A sanctuary, just like the tanning booth. Days spent in bed just to stay warm. Doing nothing, always doing nothing except one thing. Watching. Watching and cataloguing everything she saw, heard, and reacted to. Even herself. Once she got too close to the mirror, and it was as if her two eyes communicated with each other and then got stuck, pulling her down and in.

Her dormitory den mother took note of her strange behavior, and Fiona tried to act normal for her. But it was no use. She was sent to be tested fully for any psychological anomaly, and he gave her no mercy; the tester declared her

as having undifferentiated schizophrenia. All alone, Fiona
had no idea what to do. She met weekly with a psychiatrist
for a while, Dr. Pepper, who assessed her behavior and
gave her Navane, an old antipsychotic medication used to
treat schizophrenia. Then one day Fiona gave Dr. Pepper
a hug that she realized was inappropriate. She felt stupid.
Things just got worse.

She called home daily, called Celeste and Vicki daily,
and cried herself to sleep for many midmorning naps
after morning class. Classes seemed impossible, and she
began to fear them. It came down to the line. She was
going to kill herself. That would make everything easier
for everybody. That was her point of view. What was she
worth but a hit-and-run accident on the freeway?

Activated uncertainty. The inability to escape from her
own death. Pieces of paper flying in the wind, brilliant
escape as her soul stands up and clings to reality. Daddy!
Yes! Daddy will bring her home, north to Seattle, not
south where the suction of her death resided. Careening
into reality, Pa came down, and together they packed up
Fiona's room into the Bronco. Together they drove north.
Up, up, and away to a new life where everything would
be wonderful. How wrong she was. Never could there
be such a disappointing homecoming. No one was really
excited. Todd had his head stuck out the window with a
big, cheesy grin on his face, and this was both happy and
frightening for Fiona.

This old house, so empty and lonely, quiet and creaky,
full of music and footsteps. Conversation, piano. Fiona
found that the only sane way to get through a day was to

read and read profusely with tea and classical music. She took to organizing her room, a process that took place every month or so, as she made room for her electric typewriter, which took employment for a while until Dad brought home a computer for her. Fiona made room on her desk and bought her own printer, with the disabled government income she received monthly.

Keeping a daily journal was an activity that kept my mind busy other than by reading books. I, Fiona trembled when she tried to work at a job found through an older cousin. But paranoia and desperate refills of coffee made her work impossible. Answering phones was part of the job, and after four months of hell, Fiona quit. Not to say that she hadn't developed a phobia of even answering the house phone. This finally healed but then came back for other reasons, for the reasons of shame and humility of living at home and doing what appeared to be nothing but internally was a huge machine going on, processing life through it.

Now and then the huge machine would turn into an internal meat grinder, and the pain and suffering was more than Heidi, Fiona, and Sabrina together could bear. It was nauseating, suffocating, and had a hold on all of the woman's activities, as she tried to remain responsibly connected with the local mental health center and biweekly visits to Dr. Stomp Feet, her psychiatrist as mentioned earlier. Dr. Stomp Feet was wise and compromising. Wise, he listened carefully to all of her thoughts, opinions, feelings, and emotional dilemmas.

He was well tuned into what medicines were helping and which ones were harming.

Dr. Stomp Feet also served as a punching bag for all of her anger, frustrations, and humiliation.

Humiliation is a huge factor in learning how to become schizophrenic successfully. Great pain, loss, and angry liver function. Sweet, sweet desperation. Building, organizing, gathering, tossing, rejecting, using, spoiling, selling, speaking, and circulating through patterns of human behavior. Fiona, by her age, had a lot of collected information from watching and observing other people and herself relating and interrelating, reacting, and responding in as many situations as those she had witnessed. All in a growing process, always cutting meat off the bone and taking out the marrow, not wasting a bit of what she'd witnessed. Then she would put it into stew and gradually begin to stir the stew in a way that mixed all of what is human into a paramount religion of self, slowly cooking into the night, answering the question of what it is to be a human being in today's world in today's modern American society. The map could extend to other worlds, but this clownish material is solely based on the findings of all extended Dot.

Dance around, prowl and pounce like a puppy in the wind, ears flapping; this new information has made life possible for Dot. She can scream with joy and understand why people would laugh, murmur, walk away, or stare. She can fit in, stay out, run away, hide, duck, and also blend in. It is a grand-opening process that is beginning to take place as the books are written about human behavior.

Careful examination shows that her extermination and revival all tie in with a story of Christ. A blending process and a learning process to show the world the way and the wrong way. It's winning, the good side, and the bad side is weakening, based on the two personalities that kept watch and analyzed her every movement, putting her down in every occasion, saying, "Dot, you're wrong to do this," or, "You're wrong about that."

The voices march on down the road now, missing their mark, getting confused, and running into each other, embarrassed and confused. The voices in Dot's head have been so bent on destroying and repairing Dot to a museum that they've forgotten their own ways. Now the fleas start to bite. Maybe one at a time, and not many at that, but Dot is clownish enough not to laugh at another's demise, as she has had enough of such torture in her life. Life goes on, and all in all, it's going to get better for Dot. She's better, and she's learned and earned more than most jewelry stores can boast about.

Better not to show off though; that's like the giraffe that stuck its neck out and got it chopped off. How painful out there in the garden. Little by little, learning to put pieces together, she breathes quietly and relaxes a little bit more often as time goes by. Her naps are healthy, and her night rest is rejuvenating. It calls out witness to happy dreams and revealing dreams about wonderment and joy.

Happy walks and talks with Max are something she'd never dreamed could be possible. Max could be quiet and listen; he was also cute and funny, with a sense of humor that was timely for a depressed soul. Equating this, there was a soul to lift up his depressed moods and listen compassionately to the ongoing torment of voices that plagued him throughout the days.

There were "smoochers" that usually came in threes; there were "boo-hoos!" that came at a poke in the belly. And that's as far as intimacy goes here. I love him. Dot spoke. We all have our ups and downs, but together the team has impetus and staying power.

Now we get down to the encyclopedia of Dot. Dot and her hurricane of values. Her stanza of metaphors and the beauty of her delinquent mind. It's boring to be all alone, even in the darkness of night when we should be sleeping. Dot is awake, breathing into my ear, the words of the mystery. How are the fools all the clowns, and where did they go, and where did they come from? Clowns? Hippopotamus. What a religion, faith in the retarded. The element of the elephant. The campus of religion and the shadow of dying lepers who run to keep from touching the well, yelling, "Stay away. I am unclean!" It bites, but who is the front-runner for those who don't understand my way of telling?

Telling of the fortuneteller who knew the meaning of my life, and that's why I never went to see her. In a million barrels of guns, there must be one that will blow open my head, but for now I will keep on taking that serum they call water and drink it day by day, knowing it will keep me alive. Touch and go they call the rhythm recharge, and here we stand with mountains of information ready to explode into revelation. A few more sentences and I will know why. First, there is disease; then there is compilation, healing, spreading, and reaction. That's number one.

Then come freedom of religion, peace, and prosperity. Whatever makes you feel good. Make good. Be good. Do good. Arrange for goodness to come, and let goodness go.

Create happiness; take pills for stabilization, starvation, and hyperventilation when panic attacks strike. It's all real. Savage and perfunctory. Between the eyeballs, coming to a point of communication in savagery. Plain danger and letting go of self-authority. So it was, a little bit placid, but also totally invigorating if one could cancel out the pain. The ride would be amazing if that's what it would be. But not. Swamped, smothered, drowned. Sucked to death in the bottom of a hole where the snow can't get her, but the cold, nonetheless, slowly freezes her body.

Dug up and carted away, left for dead, but waking up, screaming, "My life is not over!" To the shock of all the elements, life has come out of death, or sleep. Roll over, for the shock has come that there is little fat to be had. Emaciated skin and dirty hair. What do I mean? I did it. Dot did it. She lived life to the death, doing just what she was told and knew was right. But her fears were real, and here's why. First, there was Bertha, who got raped in Singapore at eleven years old. Then, confused and bitter for her age, Carrie came along and took her place until she had to be replaced by Heidi, who could sort of get through high school and lead out from Carrie, who has her hands full protecting little Bertha and cannot grow and lead at the same time.

It's easy to see that no two colors are the same. But sometimes our eyes are mistaken, and we cannot decipher between two very similar colors. Nobody has perfect vision; there is fog down every corridor, and knock on any door, hoping to get close to your mark, because you never know if or when you will win the game of trade. Trade comes when you learn a new skill or gain new talents due to experience.

Experience gives you power, because power gives you knowledge, and knowledge shows you how. Ability comes from your side, from your own trial and error, from watching, growing, sensing, tasting, thirsting, suffering, traveling, and effort. Each clue leads you on to the next landing, where you find out how to find the next clue, and soon you've formed a vision. A vision is something you can share with anybody, at least in bits and pieces, if you want to. Your visions are yours, and they are clues as to how to live your life in any or most circumstances. Because two can look alike, it is good that we are flexible and can give birth by sharing clues and pinning down knowledge.

We are a weak species and cannot live without each other, not for long. First, there is loneliness. This is a knife that plays xylophone on your back ribs, letting you ache internally for any and all reasons when you cannot relate. Heidi, Fiona, and Sabrina have shared the most loneliness, together with each other, surrounding Dot, who pants in agony just to keep on.

The ache of loneliness turns a human being into a freak in her own eyes, thinks poor Dot. Littered with dust and papers, books and clothes, her bedroom is the one place she can hide. Hide from what? Her limitations. Her inventions, such as ways of dealing with extreme loneliness. Battering herself with questions. How to get to the bottom of this so that she might come out and see why she is so different, yet, on the surface, appear to be just the same as everyone else. Until she hides again for fear of her ugliness and rejection.

To herself she is a gigantic *clown*, someone made for people to laugh at, point at, and throw peanuts at. She should dance around and paint her face with a smile and a frown, tears, and big, smiling cheeks with a bright red nose. Curly red hair with a spotted, colorful costume...

Sabrina knows she is a clown. She cries and laughs to the extreme within one day. Or within two to three days. Sometimes depression lasts more than just a day. Heidi has seen times where her hatred fed upon her for over three weeks in misery and agony, hatred, futile life.

Brimming with tears, she hides most of them in public and lets go in her bedroom, her sanctuary.

Times have passed that made her turn on the house stereo till the windows could crack, just to take her mind off her sorrows and those evil voices that tried to convince her of being a witch, to put it mildly. Loud music and beer, because there was nobody to hang on. Nobody but her journal, and at last an interest in the Bible, which she read a little bit every day.

She searched the world of herbs and tea remedies, but

nothing really helped. There was nothing to look forward to. What kept her going she knew not, but thinking backwards now, the wonderful childhood years were so happy that she had reason to believe happiness could be achieved again, probably in a different way, but somehow, someway.

It's true that she had an illusion of finishing college and kept taking one class at a time, but she kept dropping them too. Finally, the fishhook told. Her head was no longer college material. It was too busy dealing with emotional upset and internal processing of outer input. Going to class became going to a big room with lots of noisy people and thoughts of coffee or the latest book she was reading. It was as if the class would be squeezing her out of it. So finally she stopped registering for more, but with a pacer that cried out for the right to take any class at any time if there ever be an interest. Just no more going for a degree without any declaration of a major, and that's enough.

Broken heart, not to say. Dot's not going to finish university. *It's a broken world out there,* she thinks. She can help the world in another way. She can share what she's learned along this journey of broken hearts and mutilation. Of playing the clown for the rest of her life, as a way to deal with the bad and good at once while still combing her hair, showering daily, enjoying walks, music, volunteer work, and being there to help others in need.

This would seem to wrap it up, but it opens up a whole new book. A drama, a love story, a tale of the heart and soul of a schizophrenic little girl who grew up to be a precious lady of hope, whose life is her own, who can make her own decisions, and take the blame for whatever she's done wrong, finding there is very little of that. It is the fault of the disease, not the person, and it hammers the truth into the very fact that there is no truth outside of the disease, because although they may appear so, no two look exactly alike. And they aren't.

There are medicines for specific diseases, and none acts the same on any two people. They can help, and in most cases they do, but there are cases where one person benefits from a medicine that has adverse reactions on another person. Psychiatrists have a huge job of testing and diagnosing mentally ill people. This first step must be done with care. If this initial relationship is not a positive one, it can have a detrimental effect on the diseased individual who may not want to cooperate. It is important from the outset that care be explained and a futuristic outlook outlined to give a client hope and something to cling to. Friendship with a specialist is best, especially if there can be trust and honesty, letting the whole situation be known.

If you don't trust your doctor, who can you trust? There are people who study the diseases of the mind, and there are people and medicines that treat them. Nothing is substantial, and a lot of pain and suffering must be endured, as life has to be learned to be lived all over again with a mental illness, which can strike at any time, but most often hits during the late teens and early twenties, which, of course, is the prime of life; kids are discovering what it is like to be a grownup, and they are exploring the world with their new rights and responsibilities. They are covering up for their sins and denying God, trying all sorts of bad behavior, and it is a good thing we have penitentiaries. But here the line is drawn. Was the behavior foreign of mind or premeditated? Greedy conclusions to draw. If it happens once, will it happen again?

Easter comes around once a year. At Easter we remember the resurrection of Christ. If he could forgive a criminal, can't we? If we show love, won't we receive love? True love? Not just feel-good love.

Joyful sensations can come with forgiveness, but what does all this mean? It means that the mentally ill, Dot, needs to learn to forgive the self. In this manner we are absent of all delinquency in order to keep good the feelings of the soul, something that everybody wants to keep once it has been had. Never to give up on the soul, it is your mirror of life and death in one instance.

Here you see the mirror of your soul, such as Fiona, when she looked too closely in the mirror at Stanford in her dorm and her eyes got caught up in each other, as if communicating between the two sides of her mind, wrenching herself away before her eyes got stuck. Truly her eyes were sure of themselves after that. No one knew what she was looking at anymore, for her focus could change alternately at any given moment. She had the ability to look into a crowded room and find exactly what she was looking for, but the downfall is that not one time did she know what that was.

Sickly, still. Fat. Mute. Cornered. Turn around. Run.

Escape the narrow passage, the way that her mind could see, the trail of hope…to the bathroom. That's what it's like to be all alone, afraid, worried, and on the run toward destiny and devastation as disbelieving mind with a bit of faith and a drop of hope.

Music is the front of all, the end of all, and the companion of all. It soothes emotions while words inspire and give thought to thought, for one leads to another Apparently, there is not enough to give in all situations. Those are our limits. Meet our limits. Most people don't understand their limits and just get hurt or disbelieving. Whatever the case, there is always the truth that nobody can do everything, and sharing can help connect people, especially people with significant differences.

Tattered clothes aren't always the picture of a mentally ill individual. There are those who seek and get help in as many ways as they can. Family bonds are crucial in recovery for added support and encouragement. And it is important for the diseased individual to be prepared. To know that the road ahead is rough and smooth, steep and curved, straight and full of hills. Close work with case managers and psychiatrists plus consistent pill regime are the basic ingredients for getting well.

Wellness comes when the mentally ill individual can function in society and take adequate care of the self. Each person needs to have self-control, ill or not. It is one of the hardest disciplines to cover and hold on to. It is essential in managing limitations and the disappointment found when one comes upon a limitation of the self.

Confusion is normal when we don't really know who

we are. A mixture of personalities evolved for the sake of dealing with catastrophic consequences. Bring on the battering ram and bang it on poor Dot's head. There is so much she doesn't understand. Each day she gets one day closer to her full recovery, whatever that means, probably passing the test into the next life.

And that's so far away. One tiny little second can seem so large in our gigantic universe. Touch and go, hear the flow, as trembling saturation of our own demise crumble under the destiny of our truths. Have you gone out to hurt someone? To trip them up? Or did you accidentally bump into someone in line in front of you?

Where did you come from? From "out there"? Don't forget it, because someday you'll be going back out there. Here you are just to become a better warrior, and that explains the hardships in life. Where you go when you are here is totally up to what is in your own mind and whether or not you are under control of other people. People like to control other people, but it all comes to no good.

Fragrant Fiona knows what it is to be under the control of another. The experience of multiple rapes has taught her that and earned her a clown badge on top of her mental illness. This is so sad, cries Dot, that she can hardly go on.

It is trepidation and fear that keeps her from going back, going back to Stanford. She would much like to erase it totally from her memory, for the betrayal she feels by the people who knew her there.

Not now. Fiona and Sabrina could pop up at any time

if necessary, but right now Dot likes to waver back and forth as she tries out her new wings just a little at a time. There are Dot bashers out there, so she must be very careful. Sometimes he dances near, and together they hold hands. Little Dot is graced by the presence of Max. Max, so gentle, makes no games about getting to know her. No speed, no rushing, with delicate communication methods and ultimate patience. But she must swiftly hide in time to dodge damage. Breaking bones now would be arresting. She climbs to safety and wraps herself in Fiona Clown and Sabrina Clown.

Spinning around in circles, she lands again at her old friend's doorstep, the world of books. Dot throws her books out the windows in frustration as she finds it difficult to read. So she sells some of them. Not for much. She growls at her stunted reading ability and finds out her glasses aren't of the right prescription anymore. Little things to worry about. So. There is real life. Abstract reality. The need of dental work. Things that are common to everybody. Really, Dot, look around you, and you will see your life is the same; it's just a newly discovered color, one never seen before ever.

Like blood running in rivulets down your face, your tears have turned to blood after all the hatred and pressure inside of yourself. Passion turned to peach orchards, a little sweetness to everyone who would reach out for it in respect for life. Little daisies and mushrooms growing at the base of the trees. Grassy lawns laid out among the peach trees in the sunshine, and small streams flowing nearby.

Blue skies above with white clouds billowing in the corners of the sky. Where are you? Dot dances in her imagination, and no one has ever been there except for her. Fishes in the sea, mermaids with long tails, and Heidi remembers swimming underwater with flippers on her feet, kicking up and down like a mermaid.

She remembers windsurfing and one time being caught under the sail. She remembers the eagle that chased her into the forest. And the hornets' nest she accidentally stepped on. The hornets had no mercy for her. She'd always had good runner's legs and was an excellent crew team member.

Cunning and fox-like, she learned to get what she wanted, to a limited degree. She was a psychological mystery who had hope for this world. It gave up on her, though. The world didn't believe in mysterious Dot, shrouded with Heidi, Fiona, and Sabrina. All different growth developments. Her suicide attempts to failure in resignation of the soul. Her perpetuation of insolence and gratitude for the limitation of failure. Not enough, or perhaps too much, so she needed to break new ground.

But the failure came through. How else could it appear without natural cause? Not good enough? Breaking new ground? Mental illness is real and is a road block, needing a detour. During the moment, however, leaving college appeared to be a failure, and she pounded it into herself over and over and over again. Why couldn't she go on and get a degree and graduate like everyone else? And why couldn't she have any friends?

It was horrific. Failure. In a way it is true. She failed to finish college, yet that does not incline her to be a failure in and of herself. Who hasn't failed a test at school? Is it not the end of the world? It is not. The pieces didn't fit together, whether it be family life, sickness, or many other reasons for not being prepared to score perfectly on the test.

Now Heidi got perfect grades in high school. Always. Clearly she got one "C" in trigonometry but managed to pull through the course with a resounding "A." Why then did grades deteriorate at the university in California? First of all, her four-legged support chair lost three of its legs. One, family support. Two, familiar surroundings. Three, cohesive thinking. That left one leg for her chair to balance on, self-expectations and drive.

She cared not for herself but threw herself into studies, and this worked for a while, before interesting boys began to take up much of her time. She must admit it, as she lost ability to study with her mind, she found ways to communicate with some people that took interest in her. Then the first year was over, let alone the sadness and crying due to her failure to complete classes and to maintain her first position on the freshman crew team. Sadness turned to panic as her mind continued to fail her. She could not make two ends meet. It was a bargain in the beer bin. But drunkenness did not heal her pain. It was sorrow that grew and clutched on to her, as well as a bout of mononucleosis.

Something went sadly wrong. Sabrina cried into her hands and kneeled beside her mailbox. A passerby offered help, but she declined, shaking her head, and shuddered into her hands, getting up to push her bike into a less-noticeable spot where no stranger could bother her in her insidious pain.

The prowling stranger is who she became, and she became very controlling about what she said and to whom she spoke. The cafeteria was a war zone for her, but she had to eat. So she ate.

Her bedroom was comfortable, her roommate quiet and peaceful, a Christian by the way of Jesus framed on her shelf. Fiona thinks back and realizes she was not very kind to her roommate. She stole food from under her bed and secretly envied her study habits and great ambition for undertaking course material.

Fiona went to the libraries quite often but couldn't focus there either. Her room was for sleeping and napping; nowhere could she study. Brain failure. Emotions took it hard, and soon there was so much congestion inside of her that she took the hills at the sunsets, on her bike, and rode far and wide to filter out her frustrations. She had no one to talk to. No one understood her, and she couldn't be sure of everyone else.

Sabrina declined going to dorm meetings because she hated being called on. She kept up with crew practice, and if there was ever a time of aggression being spent, it was out there on the water, where she first met God, a green light in the sky.

There is a God, she said to herself, and hope clung to her from then on, despite the dungeons and prisons that they locked her in, the people, the invaders who hurt her mind and clamored over her body like a piece of meat.

It was then that she received her own internal voice, a voice that she used to talk to herself about everything, although this grew painstakingly difficult as culture wrapped around her finger and paranoid schizophrenic became her label, not Stanford University freshman or sophomore. Breakage comes here along with a twisting of the cure, for there is no cure, just a healing.

Pills became centrifugal to all that she was, is, and ever will be. But that's okay, and all that there ever will be about it. Deep breaths and breathing over it realizes the intentions of love and life that happiness can go on, and you don't need a pizza to be happy.

Afraid of clowns? How could that be? Clowns are afraid of themselves! They scare people, they don't get close to people, and others laugh at their demise.

Yet clowns exist; they are a part of our society, and everyone has seen a clown, whether decked up or just emotionally and mentally described as happy and sad at the same time on all levels. It's a painful position, but more clowns enter our world every day. That's why there are antidepressants, and not only this, but antipsychotics too, although clowns don't necessarily need both to feel better. Some are not multi-diagnosed among the multiple psychological disorders that are recorded today.

Long ago I had the funny thought that schizophrenics wear funny clothes. To me this was true, because I had to make do. Then my tastes changed. Finally, I settled on whatever fit right, was priced right, and had tasty colors. Everything could mix together. Shoes were the most important. I don't know why, but Sabrina loves feet and has always felt a huge protection for her ankles. The last thing she wanted was a broken ankle, and medicines make her a little bit wobbly sometimes, so Sabrina likes her shoes.

Now that all those college days are over, Dot likes to go for walks, drink coffee, read, and spend lots of time thinking. She spends lots of time with Max; they like to go camping at Mt. Rainier and live in their happy home with three cats and a bearded dragon lizard named Liza.

EPILOGUE

An emotional climate has escalated from beginning to end. Hopefully you have gained some insight into the schizophrenic mind and the issues that arise out of such a helpless state. Looking onward and upward is the key to self-betterment. Enjoyment can be found, especially when limitations in life are accepted and learned, working with them to establish the level of life that is possible to attain happiness and successes, both small and large. Each learned skill allows new ones to grow. Bertha was a gift to Carrie, a catalyst for Heidi, a stronghold for Fiona, a flag for Sabrina, and a shroud for Dot. Self-defense is clearly necessary when good looks and intellect meet with limited communication abilities and social amnesia or arrested development. Safety first! Defense and aggression are tools for dealing with the dark side. It is a clue that the imagination comes first and teaches and learns. Not a fluke, life is real for everyone, delusions and all. Portrayed as an agony, life is an enigmatic journey. Take one step at a time and soon the fog clears, until you view paradise.